D1535673

WOODEN BONES

ALSO BY SCOTT WILLIAM CARTER

The Last Great Getaway of the Water Balloon Boys

WOODEN BONES

Scott William Carter

SIMON & SCHUSTER BOOKS FOR YOUNG READERS

NEW YORK   LONDON   TORONTO   SYDNEY   NEW DELHI

SIMON & SCHUSTER BOOKS FOR YOUNG READERS
An imprint of Simon & Schuster Children's Publishing Division
1230 Avenue of the Americas, New York, New York 10020

For information about special discounts for bulk purchases,
please contact Simon & Schuster Special Sales at 1-866-506-1949
or business@simonandschuster.com.
The Simon & Schuster Speakers Bureau can bring authors to your live event.
For more information or to book an event, contact the Simon & Schuster Speakers Bureau
at 1-866-248-3049 or visit our website at www.simonspeakers.com.
Book design by Laurent Linn
The text for this book is set in Minister Std.
Manufactured in the United States of America • 0712 FFG
2 4 6 8 10 9 7 5 3 1
Library of Congress Cataloging-in-Publication Data
Carter, Scott William.
Wooden bones / Scott William Carter.—1st ed.
p. cm.
Summary: Pino and his father, Geppetto, face grave danger when they are forced
to go on the run after villagers learn that a puppet made by Pino to represent
Geppetto's dead wife can move as Pino, himself, did before becoming a real boy.
ISBN 978-1-4424-2751-8 (hardcover)
ISBN 978-1-4424-2753-2 (eBook)
[1. Pinocchio (Fictitious character)—Juvenile fiction. 2. Fathers and sons—Fiction.
3. Puppets—Fiction. 4. Wood carving—Fiction. 5. Interpersonal relations—Fiction.
6. Magic—Fiction.] I. Title.
PZ7.C2482 Woo 2012
[Fic]—dc23
2011008650

FIRST
EDITION

For Katarina and Calvin

ACKNOWLEDGMENTS

Knowing that it's impossible to thank all the people who helped bring this book into being, I would like to single out a special few with the hope that those my faulty memory forgets will be forgiving. Again, at the top of the list are my trusty editors, David Gale and Navah Wolfe. Special thanks to John Silbersack, my literary agent, for his guidance and expertise. To the wonderful owners of the Historic Anchor Inn on the Oregon coast, where a chunk of this book was written: You always make me feel like family. A warm and loving thank-you to my children, Katarina and Calvin, for getting so excited when I was describing the book to you that first time. You don't know how much that meant to me. And, as always, to Heidi, my first reader, chief publicist, and partner-in-crime in life: I wouldn't be where I am today without you. Thanks for sticking with me.

WOODEN BONES

CHAPTER ONE

In the old days news traveled quite slowly. Even if something amazing happened, it still took a long time for people to hear about it. So although something extraordinary had certainly happened in this little town at the edge of a great forest, the first strange person didn't show up asking about it until nearly winter.

By then Pino had worked as an apprentice alongside his papa for nearly six weeks. It had been long enough that he'd started to forget all about his old terrible life. It had been long enough that he'd started to feel like nothing bad would ever happen to him again.

The knock came as he was learning how to sharpen the rasps, watching the master wood-carver swipe the stone across the blades with swift confidence. This made a sound that was quite loud and unpleasant, so they did not hear the knocking until the person was pounding hard on the door, startling them both.

The wood-carver handed Pino a rasp and told him to try— they were making a table—then wiped the dust and sweat off his face with a dirty rag and went to the door.

With the weather having only recently turned toward fall, they'd just begun to use the stove, keeping all the windows in the workshop shuttered after the sun went down to trap in the heat. If not, they would have seen the man coming, and Pino probably would have gotten a good look at him instead of only hearing his voice.

His papa opened the door, the man said hello, and then the wood-carver stepped into the night. Crisp air snaked into the room, sending goose bumps crawling up Pino's arms. The door was left partially open, but from Pino's vantage point he could not see either of them.

They spoke in low, murmuring voices, and because Pino was afraid to stop sharpening for fear his papa would be angry, he could not make out what they were saying. But there was something quite odd about the man's voice.

He sounded terribly sad, just as his papa used to sound before the change.

A few minutes later his papa returned. Without a word he shut the door and returned to his stool next to Pino, his head low, his curly white hair shading his eyes. The lantern on the hook above them cast long shadows throughout the workshop. His papa picked up another rasp from the table and set to work.

"Who was it, Papa?" Pino asked.

"Oh, just a man from the neighboring village."

"What did he want?"

The wood-carver focused on his work, sharpening, not looking at Pino.

"Papa?"

"To make something," his papa said gruffly.

"What?"

The wood-carver sighed impatiently and looked at Pino with a stern expression. Then, as if he was reconsidering what he was about to say, his eyes softened and he reached out and tousled the boy's hair. "Doesn't matter, Pino. It's something I can't make."

Pino had not been with the wood-carver long, but he found that comment very strange. As far as he knew, there was nothing his papa could not make out of wood.

He could make anything.

Anything at all.

It wasn't until the second strange person came calling that Pino began to get some idea of what they wanted. He and his papa were at the well, drawing a bucket of water for dinner, when they heard a mournful sound coming from the other side of the blackberry bushes—a terrible moaning that made the hairs on the back of Pino's neck rise.

Dusk had fallen, the sky was slipping into lavender, and a cold wind shriveled the leaves.

"Who's there?" his papa said. "Show yourself."

The moaning stopped. His house and workshop resided at the distant edge of the village, and so there was no one close by to help if the person in the bushes wished them harm. Pino seized his papa's rough hand. He did not know what he would do without his papa. It was too terrible to even imagine.

"Come now," his papa said, "we know you're there. Don't make me get my pistol."

Finally the bushes stirred. Out rolled a slender person in a brown cloak spotted and blotched with blackberries. The face came up, and Pino saw that it was a young blond woman, hardly more than a girl, but her face was so twisted and contorted in strange ways that she looked much older.

In the fading light Pino could not see her well, but he could still tell that she had been crying. Her cheeks glistened like the dew-coated bark of an oak.

"Signore Geppetto," she said. "Signore Geppetto, you must bring back my husband."

"What?"

"He—he was a good man. A sailor. There was an accident—he fell overboard. I miss him so terribly much."

Geppetto bowed his head. "I'm very sorry for your loss. Now, if you'll excuse us—"

"It wasn't supposed to be! It wasn't his time!"

"Yes, I'm sorry. These things happen. Now, it is getting late and my boy has not had his supper." He turned away.

"I—I know what you've told everyone, signore," the woman said. "I know you said it can't be done again. But can't you try? I will pay you whatever you want."

Geppetto headed back to the house, tugging Pino along. He gripped Pino's hand so tightly that it caused Pino pain, but Pino was too afraid to complain. The woman's face—he had never seen anything like it, so grotesque were her features. It reminded him of his bedside candle when it was burned nearly to the bottom, what remained of the wax all misshapen and lumpy.

They hadn't gone far when the woman caught up to them, grasping Geppetto's hand.

"Please," she said.

"Let go," Geppetto said.

"Please. I'll—I'll do anything."

"Let me go!" Geppetto cried.

There was a brief tussle, Geppetto managed to free himself, and then Pino and his papa fled into the house. Geppetto was sobbing, and that was almost as horrible as seeing the woman's face. Pino could not remember ever seeing his papa cry in such a way.

The woman cursed and screamed and kicked at the door. Pino was very afraid. She stayed for a long time, but eventually they heard her walk away. Pino would never forget the last thing she said, a shout from far down the road.

"We want what you have, Signore Geppetto!" she cried. "We just want what you have!"

CHAPTER TWO

"What does 'died' mean, Papa?"

Pino did not ask the question to cause trouble, but he saw right away, by the expression on his papa's face, that this was not a question like the others he had asked.

It was not like asking what it meant when food spoiled or where the sun went at night or why goose bumps formed on the backs of his arms in a cold wind. Geppetto always answered these questions with a smile. This time his papa froze, like the way a leaf in the wind froze when a fierce wind pressed it against the window.

Dinner had been eaten, the dishes washed, and Geppetto was pulling the wool blanket up to the boy's chin. Behind the closed curtains icy rain clicked against the windowpanes like someone's fingernails.

"Well," Geppetto said, as if he meant to say more, but he didn't.

"I heard that woman say it," Pino explained.

Geppetto scratched his chin. The day's stubble had formed, making the scratching rough, like the sound maple made when Papa took a plane to it. "Well, died is . . . it's like somebody not being around anymore. They're here and then they're not."

"Oh," Pino said. "Like the customers? They're here and then they're not."

"Mmm. In a way. But when someone dies, they don't come back. Not ever."

"Why don't they come back?"

Geppetto looked at Pino a long time, then rose and opened the first drawer in his dresser. He fished around until he pulled out a tiny wooden box.

It was stained a dark reddish hue, inlaid with an intricate pattern in black iron. He sat on the bed with the box in his lap, looking down on it, until finally he opened it and pulled out a yellowed sheet of paper. After contemplating it for a time, he turned it around to face the boy.

It was a sketch of a beautiful woman. Her skin was as white and smooth as finely polished ivory. Her long black hair rippled like the feathers of a raven in flight.

"This was my wife," Geppetto said. "Antoinette."

"Where is she?" Pino asked.

"Well, my boy, that's why I'm showing this to you. You see . . . excuse me, this is difficult." He swallowed and tried again. "You see, Pino, she died. So she was here and now she's not. She died in childbirth."

"Was she my mother?"

"Oh, no. The child died too. It was . . . a very sad day. But she *would* have been your mother if she were still here. She would have liked you very much."

Pino looked at the picture again. "I would have liked her too."

"I think so, yes."

"What about me?"

"What's that, Pino?"

"I wasn't here and now I am."

"Yes," Geppetto said. "Yes, that's . . . being born. In a way, it is the opposite of dying."

Pino thought about this for a while. "Is that what that woman wanted? She wanted her husband to be born?"

Geppetto smiled sadly, then ruffled Pino's hair. "You're a very smart boy—as sharp as our sharpest blade. Yes, in a way, that was what she wanted. She wanted me to make him out of wood. She thought . . . she thought this would make him alive again."

"Would it?"

"No."

Pino was quiet. Even under the covers he felt cold. He was afraid to ask the next question, but he had to know the answer.

"Papa, aren't you glad I was born?"

Geppetto's face darkened. He lifted the boy and hugged him fiercely. He smelled of sweat and woodsmoke, but it was not at all a bad smell. It was just the smell of his papa.

"Oh, my dear boy," he said, "of course. It was the best thing that ever happened to me."

"So, it would be good to be born again?" Pino said.

Geppetto pulled away, searching the boy's eyes. "Again?" he said.

"Yes," he said. He pointed at the picture in Geppetto's lap. "You could make her just as you made me. She could be born again. Then I would have a father *and* a mother. And we would all be happy."

Pino expected his papa to be delighted by this suggestion, but instead his eyes misted. He seized the boy's hands. "No, my dear Pino, you mustn't think that way. What happened to you, it was a miracle. You were once made out of wood, and now you're a real boy—only a miracle could make that happen.

That's what I have told the others, and what I will tell anyone who comes asking. It could never happen again. It would be foolish to even try. Nothing—nothing good could come of it."

"But Papa—"

"No, no, speak no more of it. It's useless to wish for something that can never be."

But Pino did think more of it. He couldn't help it.

When they were in town buying flour, milk, and other goods at the store, he saw a horse and buggy pass the store's window, kicking up dust in the sunbaked afternoon. In the seat were four people—a man, a woman, and between them, a boy and a girl. The boy and the girl were nibbling on golden brown biscotti they must have gotten from the bakery down the road.

The children looked so happy, and the man and the woman were laughing. Pino thought how wonderful it would be to have a family like that. He thought how happy Papa would be too, to have a wife who smiled and laughed the way that woman smiled and laughed.

Maybe if Pino had that kind of family, he would finally feel like a real boy. He might look like a real boy, but he never really felt like one. Sometimes when he talked with other children who came to the workshop, they would look at him in a strange way or tell him that he said funny things. He hated that. He didn't like being treated differently. He wanted to be just like everyone else.

Later that night Pino waited in bed until he heard his papa's breathing become slow and heavy, then he crept to the workshop in his nightgown. The dew-laden grass felt wet against his bare feet. He didn't dare light even a candle, but fortunately the half-moon was bright enough slanting through the windows that he needed no other light.

There, kept company only by the few chirping crickets who still lingered from summer, he set to work.

It took nearly two weeks, and by the end Pino was struggling to keep his eyes open during the day, but finally he was ready to show his surprise to his papa.

In truth, he would have liked to work on it a little longer, to apply a few finishing coats of polish, but Geppetto woke one Sunday in an exceptionally foul mood. A ferocious thunderstorm had blown in overnight, rattling the windows and shaking the roof, and Pino asked his papa if he was grumpy because of the weather.

Geppetto snapped that it would be ridiculous to be upset about a little lightning and thunder—or anything else you couldn't control, for that matter. He wouldn't say what was bothering him, but simply gazed morosely out the rain-streaked window.

He told Pino that they'd take the day off, and when Pino asked him what taking the day off meant, Geppetto shouted at the boy to go play with some of his toys and leave his papa alone.

This set Pino to crying, and then Geppetto begged forgiveness, and the two embraced. Pino waited until Geppetto went out to use the outhouse, then he hurried through the wind and rain to the workshop, returning to their cottage with his creation just seconds before his papa entered as well.

"What's that you have there, Pino?" Geppetto asked.

Pino moved away from the rocking chair, revealing the product of all his hours of labor: a life-size puppet carved with great care to resemble the sketch of Geppetto's lost wife, Antoinette.

His papa stared, eyes wide and mouth open. Pino wasn't sure if the puppet was any good, though he'd done his very best. He'd used mostly scraps, a little cherry for the arms, some elm for the neck, a few pieces of oak for the torso. But he'd gouged and chiseled and rasped every divot and mole with great care, hoping that if he did it well enough, Papa would not be angry with him for using some of their wood.

He'd had to be sneaky for the hair, shearing off some horsetail hairs when the customers were preoccupied, but he thought she came across quite well. Of course, a little paint would make her skin look even more realistic, but he could always do that later.

"Do you like it?" Pino asked.

"That—that dress," Geppetto said, his voice strangely gurgled. He brought a fist to his mouth, biting the heavily calloused skin.

"I found it in the bottom of the chest at the back of the closet," Pino said. The dress was made of red cotton with white lace, a bit wrinkled, but still pretty. "I hope it's all right, Papa. I wanted her to look just right . . . what is it? Did I do something wrong?"

"Oh, my dear boy," Geppetto said. "Oh, my dear boy, what have you done?"

"I'm sorry, Papa. I didn't—I didn't mean—"

"Do you know what today is? Today is the day my wife and unborn child died. A terrible day! I try not think of it. I—I try so very hard, and yet always, always, I remember. And now look what you've done! You create something that *forces* me to remember!"

"I didn't know!" Pino pleaded. "I'm sorry!"

"We have to take it apart."

"But, Papa!"

Geppetto brushed past Pino. He took hold of the puppet's head with both hands, his fingers digging into the horsehair.

"Papa!" Pino cried. "Please!"

"I'm sorry, boy."

Gritting his teeth, Geppetto yanked the head from side to side. It was too terrible to watch, so Pino buried his face in his hands. He kept waiting for the awful sound of splintering wood.

But then Geppetto cried out in surprise, and it was such a shock that Pino looked at what was happening.

To his astonishment, the puppet had seized Geppetto's arms, wooden fingers clamping on to his papa's wrists as sure as any vise. That wasn't all. The once immobile puppet was rising, black coal eyes blinking up at Geppetto with a face that revealed nothing. Geppetto gaped back in utter shock, fingers groping at empty air, still struggling to grab the puppet's head. The puppet moved jerkily, gears and sockets and joints stiff, but it was still much stronger than the wood-carver.

Then they were both standing, nearly eye to eye, and Geppetto fell.

He landed hard on his backside, but his gaze never wavered from the puppet looming over him. Pino went to him, but Geppetto spoke as if he didn't even know the boy was there.

"Antoinette," he whispered.

The puppet's mouth moved up and down, creaking as it swiveled on its hinges, but no other sound came out. Outside thunder boomed repeatedly across the valley, sounding to Pino much like a mallet pounding on a hollow log.

CHAPTER THREE

After that Geppetto did not speak again of destroying Pino's creation. He also never called it Antoinette, referring to it only as the puppet.

"Get that puppet out of my workshop," he'd say, or "Lock the puppet in the storeroom, Pino, I hear a wagon coming." He never looked at it when he said this. In fact, he seldom looked at it at all.

Pino begged forgiveness, but his papa told him what was done was done, and that they'd just have to see what came of it.

The puppet followed them as they went about their business, strutting and stumbling like a toddler learning to walk. It moved its mouth often, but it never spoke. Sometimes it gestured wildly with its hands, but these movements never seemed to amount to anything. It was as if the puppet felt the need to speak but had nothing to say.

When Geppetto locked it in the storeroom at night or when they had visitors, it stared at them sadly but did not resist.

Sometimes during the night Pino woke to his papa quietly sobbing. Pino never said anything, but he always had a hard time sleeping after that. He'd lie there gazing into the darkness, wondering if the puppet could hear the sound of his papa's suffering. He wondered if it would even care.

This went on for several weeks, until finally they had to go into town. Geppetto was grumpier than usual, saying he just couldn't put it off any longer. They were low on supplies.

He shoved the puppet in its closet. For once he looked it squarely in the face, pointing his rough finger just inches from the puppet's polished nose.

"Stay in here," he said. "If a customer comes while we are gone, make no sound. No one must know of your presence. Do you understand? Do you know how important this is?"

The puppet's wooden eyelids slid shut and open, but otherwise it made no response.

"Nod your head!" Geppetto said. "Do something to show me you hear me!"

Still the puppet only gaped stupidly. Geppetto slammed the door. He locked it and shoved the key into his pocket, then seized Pino's hand and tugged him out the door.

The sky was the color of a dull knife. Their breath fogged in the morning air. They'd been without a horse since their old mare died in the summer, so they had to walk. Pino was gasping for breath by the time the town came in sight.

When Geppetto saw that it was busy in town, with lots of wagons filling the streets and people milling on the boardwalks, he clenched down even harder on Pino's hand.

Geppetto was usually quite talkative with the store owner and the other customers, but this time he merely shoved the items they needed into the leather satchels they'd brought—a pound of flour, a half dozen eggs, a loaf of cheese, and some milk. Although he had less than a third of what he usually bought, he was already heading to the counter. Usually Pino asked for some licorice, but he didn't dare today.

Unfortunately, they had the bad luck to get behind Signora

Moretti, the old widow who was deaf in one ear. Her deafness hadn't impaired her love of gossip, however, and she was regaling the portly shopkeeper with news about the blacksmith's excessive drinking.

Despite Geppetto's crowding behind her and clearing his throat, she went on jabbering in her high-pitched voice, punctuated by the occasional squeal of laughter.

"Excuse me . . . ," Geppetto began.

Before he could say more, there was a great commotion outside, people along the boardwalk shrieking and shouting and crying out in surprise.

Pino was watching Papa, and he saw the wood-carver's face turn as white as the flour they were intending to buy.

Signora Moretti and the shopkeeper bustled immediately to the window, as did the others in the store. Everyone in town must have been doing the same, because there was the thumping and pounding of many footsteps on the boardwalk. Geppetto didn't move. Pino was desperate to see what was out there, but his papa had hold of him like a shackle.

"Oh my word," Signora Moretti said, a hand fluttering to her throat. "What—what is *she*?"

Geppetto's face fell, his white hair falling across his eyes like a curtain. He shook his head from side to side, then looked sadly at his boy.

"We have to move now," he said.

CHAPTER FOUR

While everyone's attention was diverted, Geppetto and Pino left the proper amount of money on the shopkeeper's counter and squeezed out the doorway. Geppetto sneaked behind the murmuring crowd that lined the boardwalk. Pino hurried after him, his satchel thudding against his back.

He caught only a glimpse of Antoinette over the wall of people, a bit of horsehair and wooden cheek. She wouldn't have seen them except that a barber standing in his doorway noticed them.

"Signore Geppetto!" the lanky man in a white apron cried, waving his razor in a way that made Pino nervous. "Signore Geppetto, is that woman your doing?"

"It's not a woman!" Geppetto shot back. "It's just a thing! It's made out of wood!"

When he spoke, the crowd shifted and turned, and for a brief moment the puppet had a clear view of them.

It stared with its dull black eyes, then immediately lurched in their direction.

Geppetto hurried even faster, racing out of town, the puppet stumbling after them like a drunk. Pino heard the whispering of the townsfolk until they passed around the first bend.

Pino begged Geppetto to slow down, but he wouldn't even answer. They put some distance between themselves and the puppet, and soon it was out of sight.

When they reached their cottage, Pino slumped to the floor, wheezing and panting. Sweat blurred his eyes. He'd never felt his heart beat so hard.

"Pack—pack some clothes for both us," Geppetto said, diving into the closet and pulling out two large sheepskin packs. "I will get whatever tools we can carry."

"But, Papa—"

"Do it!"

This sharp retort brought tears to Pino's eyes, but he fought them back. This was all his doing, so there could be no crying now.

While Papa hustled out to the workshop with one of the bags, Pino packed the other bag full of as many clothes as it would fit, leaving a little room for the food they'd just bought at the store, as well as the bread, fruit, and dried meat they still had left in their cupboard. He heard clinking and clanking from the workshop.

Only a few minutes later his papa returned. The pack slung over his shoulder bulged as if it might rip apart.

"What do you have there?" Geppetto said, glancing into Pino's bag. "You got us food—good boy. Now we should— wait, one thing more. I can't leave it."

He returned to their room and retrieved the box that contained his portrait of Antoinette. He started to put the yellowed paper into his bag, then he seemed to think better of it, folding it into quarters and stuffing it into his pant pocket.

Then he returned to the front door. He was reaching for the knob when it turned on its own and the door swung open.

Standing before them was the puppet. If not for its blinking eyes, it could have been a statue.

"You!" Geppetto cried. "How *dare* you come back here. Do you know what you've done? Do you . . . do you . . ."

His words trailed off, for he was looking over its shoulder at the road.

Pino saw the same thing as his papa: Down at the far end, just where the road bent around the corner into a grove of oaks, a crowd was fast approaching.

The dirt was still glazed with the morning frost. First it looked like just a few people, but they kept coming, dozens of them—men, women, young, and old. They filled the road like a river, flowing steadily in their direction. At first it seemed to Pino that some of them carried staffs. It was only when he looked closer that he saw that they were rifles.

Geppetto yanked the puppet into the cottage. "Get my pistol," he said.

Pino obeyed. When he returned with it, he found Geppetto shoving the puppet in the closet. Unfortunately, the doorjamb had been badly splintered during the puppet's escape, and the door wouldn't stay shut.

Cursing, Papa kicked the door a few times, then took a chair from the kitchen and braced it under the knob. By this time Pino could hear the chattering crowd. Geppetto took his pistol to the window, peering beyond the edge of a curtain. When Pino went to join him, Geppetto held up his hand.

"Stay back," he said.

The crowd grew louder; it was only now that Pino could hear the anger in the voices. Geppetto watched for a moment, then set his jaw and stepped to the door.

"No, Papa!" Pino said.

Geppetto made a motion for Pino to remain, then went outside.

Pino caught only a glimpse of the amassing storm of people, a flurry of pale faces and fogging breaths. Eyes glimmered in the frigid air, the sun glinting on shiny black barrels. Before the door shut, Pino saw that the crowd wrapped most of the way around their cottage.

"Hold there!" Geppetto cried.

There was a murmur of discontent. The closet door rattled, making Pino jump. He hurried over to it, leaning his back against the door.

"We've come for the truth!" a man shouted. It was a familiar voice, and then Pino realized it was the town's barber. "Did you create that puppet, Signore Geppetto?"

There was a moment's pause, and then Geppetto answered in a quiet voice. "Yes, I did."

Another murmur rose from the crowd, this one more excited than angry. Pino did not understand why his papa would lie.

"But it was a grave mistake," Geppetto said. "It can't be done again."

"Liar!" a woman shouted.

"Go home!" Geppetto cried. "Go home and forget all this nonsense!"

"Don't be greedy, wood-carver!" another man said. "We just want our loved ones back!"

"It can't be! Go away!"

Later Pino would have a hard time remembering exactly how it started. There was lots of shouting back and forth. Someone fired a gun. Perhaps it was Geppetto, firing into the sky to try to scare them off, or perhaps someone in the crowd twitched a trigger finger by mistake, but then lots of bullets were flying.

Windows smashed and the glass rained down all around them. Geppetto fired back, aiming high, but then a bullet sliced into his shoulder.

He cried out in agony and slumped to the floor, pressing his hand against the blood blooming on his shirt.

"Papa!" Pino cried, rushing to him.

They crouched on the floor beneath the window. Bullets still plowed into the cottage, smashing glasses in the cupboard and a vase on the table.

A flaming torch sailed through a broken window and immediately set fire to their rug. Then another sailed through and landed on the table. Smoke filled the room, stinging their eyes and choking their lungs.

"What're we going to do?" Pino said.

Geppetto looked at him. For the first time in his short life Pino saw that the man who had made him, the man who had fashioned him out of wood and given him life, did not always have the answer. Before he had much time to think about it, the closet door banged open and the puppet lurched into the hazy room, stopping when it saw them, oblivious to the flaming carpet beneath its feet.

"Move!" Geppetto said. "Don't just stand there, Antoinette!"

But it was too late. Pino had made her out of old wood, the kind that has had months to dry and become rich food for a hungry fire.

The flames exploded up her legs, lighting her dress as if it were newspaper. Only when she was completely engulfed did she seem to realize what was happening, and then she ran around in circles, flapping flaming arms.

It was at that moment that Pino realized a way to escape. With the walls burning and crackling all around him, and bullets still flying, he lunged for the door. He threw it open, staying out of sight of the crowd.

"Pino!" Geppetto said. "No!"

"Antoinette!" Pino shouted. "Go to the well! It'll put out the fire!"

For a moment Pino didn't think it would work. The flaming puppet continued its mad pirouettes.

But then it stopped, looked at Pino with its black eyes encased in shimmering flames, and ran for the door. As soon as the dull thuds of its feet reached the deck, the sight of the puppet—fully afire, lurching crazily, waving its arms—had the effect Pino wanted.

A woman screamed. Then another. The gunshots stopped, and then there were the sounds of people fleeing. "A monster! A monster!" the people cried.

"Let's go, Papa!" Pino said.

They grabbed their bags and fled out the door, using the cover of the smoke and the crowd's hysteria to escape to the forest unnoticed.

Geppetto's right arm was as red as if he'd dipped it in a barrel of paint. Before disappearing into the trees, Pino took one last glance back at the mayhem surrounding what had been the only home he had ever known—the flaming roof of their cottage, the smoky outlines of people fleeing, and the shrieks and screams rising up from the townsfolk who had once been Geppetto's loyal customers.

The last thing Pino saw, before they vanished into the forest, was the flaming puppet of Antoinette running in circles in front of the cottage, grasping at the air as if she were trying to hug someone who wasn't there.

CHAPTER FIVE

All their running took Geppetto and Pino deep into the woods surrounding their home. If you've ever been truly frightened—not just startled or surprised, like you might feel when someone pops out of a closet as a sort of joke, but truly frightened—then you know exactly how Pino felt in that moment.

You know what it's like to be so scared that your heart is a loud drum in your ears; to be so scared that every snap of a twig and every moving shadow is your enemy; to be so scared that your mind itself feels like it's on fire.

Run! They're coming! They're going to get us!

Those were the only thoughts going through Pino's mind. If he'd been paying attention, he never would have chosen to flee into the dark woods—and certainly not the woods that lay to the west, which were the darkest of all. The canopy of trees thickened until nearly all the morning light was squeezed from the world and the way ahead was steeped in shadows. It wasn't long before the sound of their burning cottage was left far behind, replaced by an eerie silence that was broken only by the snap of twigs from their footsteps or by their own haggard breathing.

The air cooled, moisture beading on their faces. A wispy fog curled around mossy stumps and pooled in shallow ravines.

The trees—they began to look less healthy. Some were bent and stooped like old men. Others looked withered, sporting few leaves.

They ran still farther, and the trees were not only bent and withered, but blackened and charred as well. A great fire had obviously swept through the woods long ago—one that had burned so deeply that the forest had still not recovered.

It was a dead and lonely place.

Finally Geppetto collapsed on a bed of half-rotted ferns, gasping for breath. He pressed a hand against his wound and clenched his teeth. The blood dripped between his fingers and smeared the wet leaves.

"Papa!" Pino cried.

"It's—it's all right, boy," Geppetto said. His cheeks were so pale that they made Pino think of the whitest elm. "Just—just need to rest . . . a moment . . ."

"But they're coming!"

Geppetto shook his head. "No. Not here. They won't come in here."

"Why not?"

"Because . . . because we're in the bad woods, boy. People—people don't go in here. Not ever."

He tried to say more but then lost the words in a fit coughing. Pino glanced behind them. With his heart still pounding in his ears, he wouldn't have been able to hear people coming even if they were, but he didn't *see* anyone. At least not with any certainty. The tapestry of shadows in their wake made it seem as if there were both hundreds of people crouching back there—and no one at all.

When he looked back at Geppetto, he was alarmed that his papa's eyes were closed.

"Papa?" he said.

Geppetto remained motionless. Pino tried to speak again, but his throat tightened and choked off the sound. Could he have lost his papa already? It was not fair, not fair at all. Other boys and girls got to be with their papas for many years. Pino could not lose him. He wouldn't know what to do. He wouldn't know how to take care of himself.

Papa might be gruff and moody at times, but he was a good papa. On the slow days he would often take Pino fishing at the pond. He always made Pino's tea just the way he liked it, with extra lemon. And during thunderstorms he never complained when Pino crawled into bed with him, not even once. He was a good papa.

Pino didn't want to lose him.

He didn't want to be alone.

Cautiously, afraid of what he was going to find, he touched the side of Geppetto's face. He was afraid the flesh was going to be as cold as a winter stone, but it wasn't. It was still warm. He held his fingers over Geppetto's open mouth . . . waiting . . . hoping . . . and felt a breath.

"Papa?" Pino said. "Papa, can you hear me?"

Geppetto murmured. It was hardly any sound at all, only the slight movement of air through the throat, but it made Pino's heart leap for joy. He hugged him, not even caring that the blood would seep into his own clothes.

"Papa, Papa!"

"So very . . . tired . . ."

"You *must* wake up, Papa. We can't stay here."

"Tired . . ."

It took enormous effort, but Pino shifted Geppetto to a sitting position. It was like trying to pull up a sack of potatoes;

his papa didn't have any strength of his own. His head drooped to the side, the white hair falling in front of his face.

"Papa," he said, "Papa, we have to go. You have to get up now. Please get up." He knew they couldn't stay there long. His papa needed help from someone who could give it. Without it, he really would die. "Please, Papa, I need you to get up."

"Huhnnn . . ."

"Can you get up?"

"Up . . ."

"Papa—"

"Antoinette?" Geppetto murmured. "Is that you?"

The name sent a chill creeping up Pino's spine. Since he was behind Geppetto, he could not see his face, but he could see that Geppetto's head was no longer rolling aimlessly from side to side—it was fixed, pointed toward an area of the forest where the shadows were deepest. He was obviously looking at something, but there was nothing there.

Then Pino saw it—a pair of red eyes emerging from the dark.

The eyes glowed like hot embers from a fire. They grew brighter and larger, until the light from the eyes themselves illuminated a long snout and oily black fur. A wolf. Not just a wolf. A *giant* wolf, nearly as big as a horse, it seemed. The snout opened, baring rows of jagged teeth. Except for the red eyes and the white teeth—which seemed to float, suspended, in the shadows—the rest of the beast blended with the dark forest around it.

The wolf greeted him with a low, rumbling growl that raised the hairs on the back of Pino's neck.

"Antoinette?" Geppetto said.

"No, Papa." Then, to the wolf, Pino shouted: "Go away! We don't want you here!"

The growling stopped, but the eyes went on staring.

"Leave!" Pino cried.

When the wolf still wouldn't go, Pino felt the panic rising up within him, like a flurry of hornets stirring inside his stomach. It could not end here. Not like this—eaten by a wolf. Didn't they have enough troubles? It made Pino angry, and the anger gave him a surge of courage. He spotted a stone, one big enough to do some damage, and without hesitation he snatched it up and hurled it at the wolf.

The stone sailed far over the wolf's head, but the act seemed to take the wolf by surprise. It gaped at them as if it didn't know what to do.

"Leave!" Pino cried again.

When the wolf merely blinked, Pino picked up another stone and threw it. And a third. And a fourth. With the fourth his aim was better, and he winged the wolf's pointed ear.

The wolf yelped and scurried away, the red eyes fading into the darkness.

Pino felt victorious. He'd stared down a menacing threat and forced it to go away. Now he turned his attention to his papa, who was again slipping into unconsciousness, peering up at him through slit eyelids. Pino grabbed him by his bloodied shirt. It took all the strength he had—his arms straining, his legs threatening to buckle—but he managed to get Geppetto to his feet.

The fog curling between the trees thickened. What little light remained in the forest drained away, leaving the world darker than before.

"Papa," Pino pleaded, "we have to go back. Get help for you."

Geppetto groaned. Pino started to lead him back the way they'd come, but that seemed to rouse Geppetto—he bucked upright, resisting.

"No, no," he said, "can't go back—no, they'd kill us."

"But Papa—"

"They—they hate us, boy. Done with those folks. Done forever . . ."

"We need the doctor!"

"Another town. Another—"

"Where?" Pino cried. "Which way? Tell me."

But Geppetto had no answer. If his papa did not know the way to another town, then Pino saw only one solution—return home. Of course, Pino couldn't think of it as home anymore, not after the way they'd been treated, but there was a doctor there. A man who could help. Pino again tugged Geppetto in the direction they'd come, and again Geppetto offered resistance. But this time the resistance was short lived, and he reluctantly agreed to be led.

They'd taken only a few stumbling steps, though, when Pino again heard a menacing growl from the darkness.

A pair of red-glowing eyes flared in the shadows ahead of them. Grew brighter. Pino cast around for another stone, but then another pair of eyes appeared. A second growl joined the first. Then a third pair of eyes blinked open, and the growling became a rumbling chorus. Soon dozens of red eyes spotted the way ahead, like a wall of angry fireflies.

No amount of stones would be enough.

They had to run.

Which was what they did—turning and sprinting in the opposite direction. The thunderous growling gave Geppetto a jolt of new life. At first he limped, holding his shoulder, but then he seemed to forget all about his wound and ran with the swiftness of a much younger man, grabbing Pino's hand and tugging him along. Pino had never seen him run so fast.

Behind them the growling gave way to snarling, and to the angry footsteps of dozens of hungry pursuers.

Geppetto dropped their bags, hoping that would satisfy the wolves, but they ignored them. When Pino stumbled, Geppetto swept him up in his arms. They swerved around rotting stumps and leaped over foggy ravines. Glancing over Geppetto's shoulder, Pino had a clear view of the pursuing pack of wolves—their red eyes dancing up and down over the uneven terrain, their ragged fur bristling in the wind, their misshapen bodies flitting in and out of the shadows.

They were gaining.

One trailing jaw snapped at Geppetto's heel, narrowly missing. Another lunged for Pino's hand, clamping down on the air just inches from Pino's fingers. Another few seconds and the whole pack would swarm over them—and then suddenly Pino was sailing into the air, having been hurled upward by Geppetto.

A tree.

He sailed into a tree—or what was left of a tree, a massive old oak that had been blackened by a fire, its scorched limbs bearing not a single leaf. It stood in a ring of other blackened and withered oaks, the biggest of the bunch, its creaky limbs bent and twisted in every possible angle, as if it had been searching in its dying days for light it could never find. Pino just managed to grab the crumbling lower limb, scrambling up, pieces of bark raining below.

Geppetto was only an instant behind. He wrapped both arms around the limb and began to heave himself up next to Pino.

Before Geppetto could pull himself to safety, a wolf lunged in the air—and clamped its jaws around Geppetto's pant leg.

The weight of the snarling beast tugged Geppetto down. He was slipping. Pino grabbed his papa by his shirt, leaning backward against the trunk of the tree. Even with his added weight, the wolf was winning, Geppetto's grip beginning to give. If Pino didn't let go, they would both go down.

But he wasn't letting go.

Not ever.

Another wolf lunged and bit into Geppetto's legs, and this time the teeth found flesh. Geppetto cried out. But in the process the second wolf bumped the first, causing it to swing like a pendulum, and the added force tore Geppetto's pants. There was a great rip and both wolves sailed clear.

Pino took advantage of the moment to pull his papa to safety—an instant before another pair of snapping jaws sailed past the place where Geppetto's foot had been.

They scrambled up the limb on hands and knees, Geppetto wincing at his wounded ankle. It was such a wide trunk that they could sit shoulder to shoulder against it, their knees pressed to their stomachs, their feet resting where the branch met the trunk and the flaking black wood was thickest.

The furious wolves lunged and snapped their jaws, white teeth flashing just above the limb, but none could reach them. For the moment they were safe.

This thought had no more occurred to Pino then one of the wolves got a new idea. Instead of trying to attack Geppetto and Pino, it attacked the dying tree—leaping against it and springing away with all four paws. Pino had no idea why it would do this, until he heard a terrible sound.

The creak of protest from the old oak.

Another wolf did the same. Then another. This would have had little effect on a big, healthy oak, but it was too much for a dying one. The tree groaned. A steady procession of wolves, rabid with desire, pummeled the charred trunk. There was the sound of crackling wood. The oak swayed.

Leaned.

Tipped.

Geppetto hugged Pino around the shoulder, pulling him close. Pino looked to his papa for comfort, but Geppetto had gritted his teeth and pressed his eyes shut.

The tree began to fall.

CHAPTER SIX

For the briefest of moments Pino himself gave up. Like his papa, he closed his eyes and resigned himself to their fate, for there seemed no way out of their terrible predicament. The tree would fall, and if they managed to survive that part of it, the wolves wouldn't let them live for long.

Then, in the rush of wind through his hair, Pino was struck with an idea. And this time it was he who spoke the name of Geppetto's long-lost wife.

"Antoinette," he whispered.

Somehow he'd given her life—not the real woman, of course, but the thing he'd fashioned out of wood scraps and horsehair. Somehow he'd performed a miracle, breathing life into a lifeless puppet, giving strength to something that had lacked any will of its own. Not a life like theirs, surely, but *some* kind of life, so why couldn't he do it now? Why couldn't he do it when it mattered most?

The problem was he didn't know how.

As the falling tree picked up speed, Geppetto clutched him tightly. Opening his eyes, Pino repeated the same thought again and again in his mind: *Come alive! Come alive! Come alive!*

Still the tree fell, the dark forest resounding with the wrenching and crackling of the old trunk; dirt clouded the air like ash; withered roots sprang from the ground like frightened worms. Down it went. Down to its doom. All that Pino could think—even while he continued wishing ardently for the tree to come alive—was how this was all his fault.

If he hadn't been born, none of this would have happened.

It was a terrible feeling—guilt and rage and regret all mixed into one, wrapped in a blanket of empathy for the only person he'd ever loved. He didn't care about himself. He just didn't want his papa to die.

At the last moment, when Pino saw the ravenous red eyes of the wolves rising to greet them, something quite extraordinary happened.

The tree took a step.

It took a step in the same way that *anyone* would take a step if someone gave him a push from behind—a lunging step that prevented it from falling. A hop onto one foot. A stumble with all the weight on one knee.

Instead of one solid trunk below, there were now two—half had split off and formed a blackened leg on which the tree rested.

There was more creaking and crackling. Pino felt a terrible shudder ripple through the trunk, and for a moment he feared that the decaying wood would not bear the weight of the tree and they would still go down. But then a second leg ripped from the ground, muddy earth exploding around them, and stepped beside the first. The old oak straightened. The leafless limbs, a cloud of bent and warped twigs that snapped at the slightest touch, coalesced and merged into what resembled two black, sinewy arms.

This development only further enraged the wolves. Snapping and slashing in their fury, they lunged at the tree. Their claws ripped through crumbling bark; their teeth broke off chunks of disintegrating branches. The air was a haze of black—a blur of oily fur and plumes of bark bits. Red eyes streaked the haze.

The old oak fought back, swinging wildly at its attackers with its bulky arms. Though the tree was slow, occasionally a swing made contact, and a howling wolf went spinning through the air. Bits of branches and bark went spinning right along with it.

Pino and Geppetto held fast to each other and the trunk. Though the tree was fighting valiantly, Pino knew it would only be a matter of time before the wolves won the battle. There were just too many of them and the tree was in such bad shape for it to turn out any other way.

As long as they stayed.

That was Pino's sudden realization. Since the tree now had legs, it didn't *have* to remain in the same spot, did it? He leaned close to the trunk, lips brushing against the gritty bark.

"Run," he whispered.

The tree went on fighting, flailing at the wolves. The wolves had figured out how to time their leaps to avoid the slow-moving arms—splitting themselves into two groups, one side distracting the tree while the other lunged.

"Run," Pino said again.

This time the tree heeded his command. When the wolves leaped again, instead of swatting them, the tree leaned out of the way and let the wolves fly past. The tree turned west, where the forest grew darker, and took a step. Then another. Then it was running, one thunderous footstep at a time.

Riding atop this charging monstrosity reminded Pino of the stories his papa sometimes read him, stories about brown-skinned people in hot deserts in faraway lands. As he gripped the tree's trunk, holding on for dear life, Pino imagined that riding piggyback on the charging tree must be much like riding an elephant in those stories. It was so big and powerful that you were completely at its mercy.

Unfortunately, the wolves wouldn't be so easily detoured. They quickly fell into pursuit, snapping at the tree's root-entwined heels.

Bits of bark broke free and spiraled in the tree's wake, swirling into the fog that blanketed the forest floor. As it lumbered, the tree swung at the wolves, warding them off, but the wolves were much better at running than the tree. If anything, they had a greater advantage during a chase than when the tree was standing still.

Worse, as the path before them grew darker, it also thickened—the dying trees were closer together, the shriveled branches extended farther into their path. The charging tree plowed through crackling walls of wood, many of its own branches breaking free. More than once Pino had to duck to avoid being whacked in the face.

Each booming footstep echoed through the forest. The ground tilted; they were descending. It was so hard to peer ahead in the gloom that Pino didn't see the steep ravine—at least a hundred-foot drop to a creek filled with jagged rocks—until they were right on top of it.

"Stop!" he cried.

But it was too late. The tree, never breaking stride, jumped. The wolves jumped after it. For a few seconds all footsteps were silent, and there was no sound but the faint whistle of wind through withered branches and wet fur. The creek beneath them shimmered through the fog like a blade under a thin white sheet.

The fog was so thick, and the light so poor, that Pino couldn't even see the other side—until the tree's root-wrapped foot boomed into the dirt. A second boom followed, and then the tree was running again. Dozens of galloping paws followed.

There was no time even to breathe a sigh of relief, for the wolves immediately resumed their attack.

It didn't seem possible, but the trees on this side of the ravine were even blacker and uglier than the ones on the other side. They closed tight around them, forming a tunnel, the dry bark woven like snake skins. The tunnel narrowed until finally all the shadowy gaps between the branches disappeared—they'd reached a wooden wall.

The tree smashed through it.

As it did, it lost half its remaining branches. The other side was quite a bit different: a cliff face of shiny black rock, and at the base of that cliff a deep darkness that must be the mouth to a cave.

It was the darkest cave Pino had ever seen.

Until he saw that cave, he had never known something could be so dark. It was as if light itself was turned aside when it reached the cave, barred entry like an unwelcome guest. Even looking at the cave, Pino felt afraid. It was not big enough for the tree, but it would be more than big enough for people, if anyone was dumb enough to venture inside.

The tree had unwittingly trapped itself, blocked on one side by the cliff and the other side by the dense wall of dying trees. The only way out was the way it had come in, and the wolves must have realized this, for they staged all their attacks while shrewdly guarding the passage out.

One after another the wolves propelled themselves at the tree, attacking in a frenzied storm, not giving the tree a chance to defend itself. While the tree whacked one wolf away, another five tore it asunder. There wasn't much left of it—just the hint of a charred skeleton, wolves tearing at its legs, gripping on to its arms. The extra weight made it stumble backward.

As the dark mouth in the cliff face loomed, Pino saw their opportunity. Remain, and they would surely die. Jump, and they had a chance. They could take refuge in the cave. Who knew what lay within, but whatever it was, it had to be better than holding fast to a tree that wasn't going to be a tree much longer.

"Jump!" he yelled.

There was no time to say more, but fortunately Geppetto recognized what Pino meant. When the tree was leaning far back, only a few feet from the lip of the cave, they both jumped. Pino landed hard on smooth black rock but managed to roll to his feet. Geppetto, with his gimpy ankle, did not fare as well; he crumpled into a ball, crying out in pain.

Sensing easy prey, the wolves came at them, but the tree focused its remaining strength on protecting them, batting away each snarling attacker. Pino scrambled to his papa and helped him to his feet.

As they limped into the cave, Pino glanced over his shoulder. The spectacle that he saw made his heart heavy. The tree was swinging and flailing and smashing everything around it, but there were just too many sharp claws and jagged teeth. The red eyes glowed hotter with rage; the snarling and growling grew deafening as the end was at hand. What remained of the tree disintegrated in front of Pino's very eyes, an explosion of splintering wood that turned the tree into something else.

Something that *had been* rather than something that *was*.

His heart felt heavy because it was the second time Pino had given something life only to watch it be destroyed.

Then, as the red eyes turned upon him, searing the air with hunger and desire, he plunged into the cave.

CHAPTER SEVEN

It was not just a dark cave. It was a *cold* cave, much colder than it had a right to be. Creeping forward, Geppetto leaning against him, Pino had taken only a few steps when he felt the cold seeping into his bones. He felt the deep darkness stealing his heat with every step, leaving him feeling like brittle ice.

The ground was uneven, scattered with damp boulders and slick stones. One wrong step and he might stumble; if he stumbled, he would most certainly shatter. That's what happens to ice.

His eyes were open and unblinking, but they might just as well have been closed, for all the good they did. He felt strange too—a strangeness he could not explain, like he was somewhere he didn't belong.

The air smelled dank and foul, as if wet, rotting things had been left there long ago and the smell remained. If he'd had a choice, he most certainly wouldn't have pressed onward, but the sudden baying of the wolves behind him—a frustrated, almost mournful sound—was like a poker pressed against his back. The wolves howled and whimpered and scratched at the stones at the mouth of the cave, but they did not follow. It was Pino and Geppetto's first sign of good luck, if you could call hurrying into such a queer, dark place good in any sense.

Each time Geppetto stumbled, Pino helped him along, but the stumbles became more frequent. Pino's strength was failing him. The way was so black that he had to grope forward like a blind man, trying to avoid smashing their heads on any unseen jutting stones. Geppetto's raspy breathing echoed off the cave walls. The passageway narrowed.

When they rounded a corner, a sliver of daylight appeared in the distance—like a single golden hair afloat on a pool of oil. Pino blinked a few times, thinking it was a trick of the eye, but the light remained.

"Must . . . rest, " Geppetto said, his teeth chattering. "So tired."

"Just a little farther," Pino said.

"Tired. So very . . . tired."

Pino thought it was going to take them quite a while to reach the golden light, since it appeared a long way off, but they reached it in seconds. The sliver of light wasn't small because it was far away; it was small because it was a sliver.

A narrow shaft of daylight shone down from a needle-size crack far above, painting a tiny yellow oval the size of a coin on the slick gray stone below. It wasn't much, but the very sight of the daylight warmed Pino's soul. It was a sign of a better world, of a better place, one not strangled by all the darkness and all the cold.

Geppetto stumbled into the light, falling flat on his stomach, his breathing fast and shallow.

"Rest now," he sighed.

"Papa!" Pino said. "Papa, you *must* get up."

Even with Geppetto's face fully under the shaft of light, he was still mostly shrouded in darkness. All the pink was drained from his cheeks, the skin like parched and bleached granite. He looked up at Pino through slit eyes.

"This . . . this is the end for me, boy," he said.

"No!" Pino shot back.

"I'm sorry. I can't . . . I can't go on."

"You can! You must!"

"I love you, son."

"Papa!"

"Hug me now." There was an odd quaver in Geppetto's voice. "Hug me close. I want to feel your warmth on me. My boy . . . my only son . . ."

"Papa!"

Geppetto didn't answer, the pauses between each raspy breath growing longer. Pino pressed himself against Geppetto, wrapping his bony arms around his papa's chest and hugging him tight. His body seemed so big in comparison to Pino's thin little arms, like the trunk of a sturdy tree; it didn't seem possible that he could die. Big, sturdy trees didn't die, did they? And he was warm, too. If he were dying, he wouldn't be warm. He would be cold, as cold as the cave.

Pino leaned close to Geppetto's lips. He felt warm breath on his ear—faint, but still there. He was definitely alive, at least for a little while longer.

"*Pinocchio . . .*"

The sound didn't come from Geppetto. It was so weak that Pino at first thought he'd imagined it—or if he hadn't imagined it, that it was just some hiss of the wind against wet stones.

"*Pinocchio . . .*"

The second time Pino recognized it for what it was—a voice. A lilting woman's voice, whispering his name. His full name. The name his papa had given him in the early days, before the change. It was the name he'd used for a long time, before his papa decided that such a long name was too much of a mouthful for everyday use. That's when he'd become Pino, and that's what he'd gone by ever since.

"Pinocchio . . . come closer . . ."

The sound was definitely coming from up ahead, deep within the darkness. Pino did not want to leave Geppetto. It didn't seem right, leaving him alone. But he felt the beckoning call of the voice. It was irresistible. He *had* to know.

"Come closer. . . ."

The voice wasn't human. It sounded human, but Pino could tell right away that it wasn't. It was something else. Something magical.

Magic.

If it was magic, maybe it could help his papa. Maybe it could make him better. That would be worth risking leaving his papa alone. Besides, what other choice did he have? He could go back to the entrance, but he was sure the wolves would still be waiting. And even if they weren't waiting, it would take far too long to return to their village.

After giving Geppetto's arm a squeeze in parting, he edged forward, leaving the narrow band of light behind. The way ahead was pitch black. He crawled over damp stones and dry stones, smooth stones and rough stones. He crawled through wide-open spaces and passageways so narrow he had to turn sideways. He crawled for minutes or hours or days, he could not tell. He crawled until his chapped hands, rubbed raw by the rock, came up against a wall.

It was as smooth as glass. He felt around it, but he found only a single, narrow hole, not even big enough for his hand. The hole was just as smooth as the rest of the wall. He was staring at this hole—or at least where he thought the hole was, for it was so dark he couldn't see a single thing—when a jet of musty air shot out of the hole and blasted him in the face.

"Pinocchio . . ."

This time the voice was much louder, and it so startled Pino that he fell on his back. A smudge of blue appeared, illuminating the border of the hole. It started as a soft, warm light, but it grew brighter, more intense, spilling out of the hole like electric smoke. The light swirled around him, undulating eddies buffeting the air, accelerating, spinning faster and faster—brightening the tiny cavern in which he found himself, bathing the black rock with blue light.

Inside the shimmering light, shapes began to appear. At first they were no more than blots of color, ghostly wraiths blooming and disappearing as if he were inside a twisting kaleidoscope. Then the images sharpened. They appeared only for a moment before vanishing into a swirl of blue, but it was enough—Pino froze when he saw what they were.

Geppetto standing next to a smiling redheaded woman, one who wasn't Antoinette . . .

Pino, as a lifeless puppet, sitting on Geppetto's workbench, gathering dust . . .

Pino crying over the dead body of Geppetto in this very cave . . .

Geppetto and Pino on the deck of a great ship, nothing but ocean all around . . .

Geppetto standing on a scaffold while a noose was fitted around his neck . . .

The same images kept appearing and reappearing. Many of them Pino recognized from his own memories, but the others . . . what could they be? He'd never been on a ship in his life, and he'd certainly never seen Geppetto with a noose around his neck.

Suddenly the woman's voice spoke again: "What you see is all that *was* and all that *wasn't*, all that *will* be and all that *might* be. . . ."

The voice came from all around him, as if the woman was spinning with the images inside the light. Pino, propped up by his elbows, leaned forward and hugged his knees. "Who are you?" he asked.

There was a pause, and then: "I have no name."

"What do you want?"

"To help you," the woman said. "I can be heard only by those with special gifts, and here is my message to you, dear Pinocchio. As long as you are true to yourself, your heart will never harden, and the future is yours to shape."

Pino had no idea what this meant, and at the moment he really didn't care. He cared about only one thing. "I want to save Papa," he said. "Can you help?"

The spinning blue light began to slow. The light itself began to fade.

"Please!" Pino begged.

"Find the girl with no arms and no legs," the woman said.

"Where?"

The light was gone, leaving Pino once again alone in the darkness. He thought that was it, that no more help would be forthcoming, but then there was one final whisper: *"Go north to Sapphire Lake. . . . Farewell. . . ."*

With that, the voice was gone, and the cave seemed even colder than it was before. Pino was also quenched with a terrible loneliness; he had never felt so lonely, not even in the days before the change, when he was on his own. His breathing—which had become ragged without his realizing it—echoed off the rocks crowding around him.

All that will be . . . The woman's warning filled him with panic. By showing him crying over his papa, was she saying it was already too late to save him? Why tell him to find this girl if it wouldn't matter? It would be a cruel trick.

Returning to Geppetto, Pino twice banged his forehead on some low stalagtite, but he didn't stop, his own heartbeat a roar in his ears. Finally he saw the sliver of yellow light—and there was his papa, lying prone just as Pino had left him. The light shone on his motionless face.

"Papa," Pino said.

There was no reply. Pino leaned over him and put his ear against Geppetto's lips. He waited. And waited. And waited some more—and *still* there was no breath.

It was true, then.

His papa was dead.

A strange, gurgled moan rose up from the darkness, a terrible noise from some terrible creature, and it scared Pino until he realized that the sound was coming from within him. His eyes blurred with hot tears. What a terrible way for his papa to die—alone, in the dark. This wasn't supposed to happen. Mixed with Pino's sorrow was a gathering rage—rage at having been so cruelly deceived. Why give someone hope if there was no chance at all?

"Oh . . . ," Geppetto sighed.

Pino jumped. He wiped away the moisture in his eyes. "Papa?"

"Mmm . . ."

"Papa! Papa!"

"My boy . . ."

The eyelids cracked open. Pino hugged Geppetto fiercely. When he spoke to Geppetto again, there was no reply—but there *was* a rush of warm air escaping his lips. It had just been so faint he hadn't felt it before.

There was hope after all. Pino hated to leave, but he had no choice; his papa was far too heavy to carry.

Pino could do one thing for him, though. He unbuttoned his own shirt—it was badly torn and bloodied from all their ordeals, but it was still something—and draped the thin fabric over his papa's body. The cold air clenched Pino's naked chest and made his teeth chatter worse than before, but he didn't care. He was going to run so fast he wouldn't even notice.

"I'll be back soon," he said, then scooted into the darkness.

CHAPTER EIGHT

The wolves were gone.

When Pino reached the mouth of the cave, all that was waiting for him in the clearing—a clearing that had darkened considerably—was a pile of scorched branches that had once been part of the tree they'd ridden to safety. Lying there on the jagged gray stones, the branches did not move or quiver; all the life had gone out of them. No red eyes glared at him from the narrow gaps between the oaks that encircled the area. No growls rose out of the wispy fog.

A few lonely crickets chirped. A solitary owl, somewhere quite distant, hooted a somber warning.

Pino, afraid the wolves were lying in wait in the shadows, would have waited much longer, but there was no time. Every moment was precious.

The problem was, he wasn't sure which direction to go. The voice in the cave had told him to go north, to Sapphire Lake, but which way was north? The cliff formed an impregnable wall behind him. What little sky he could see above him was a deep, impenetrable gray. No sun could be seen. The trees cast no shadows—at least no distinct shadows, for there were shadows everywhere.

A cool wind stirred dust along the barren stones outside

the cave, sweeping across Pino's bare chest and blowing back his hair. He shivered. Gooseflesh formed on the backs of his arms.

The seconds were ticking away.

Inside the cave Geppetto was dying.

North, north—how could Pino tell which way was north? He hurried to the thick trunks that formed a wall around the clearing, stepping through the gap created when their tree had barreled through them.

He remembered his papa telling him that moss often grew thickest on the north side of the tree, but what little moss he could find seemed to grow evenly on all sides. He also remembered how the top branches of many trees grew more consistently in an easterly direction to catch the first morning light, something his papa had told him once, but inside the dense forest Pino couldn't see the tops of the trees. It was as thick as a roof, made worse by the fading light and the heaviness of the air.

The tops of the trees.

This gave Pino an idea. He might not be able to tell the direction from down here, but maybe he could up higher.

Picking the tallest tree, one with plenty of branches from top to bottom, not an oak but some kind of pine, he started climbing. He hated to waste so much time, but it would be much worse if he chose a certain direction only to find later he'd chosen wrong.

The rough bark chaffed his hands, hands already raw from crawling through the cave. The higher he climbed, the thinner the branches became. He had to be careful. Many of the slender ones broke off at his touch; others scratched at his back and chest. Soon he was covered with dozens of cuts.

He climbed and he climbed and soon he was exhausted, his

arms and legs painfully throbbing, but each time he thought of resting, he only had to think of his papa to get a new burst of energy. Bits of bark rained down on his face and pricked his eyes. Dry needles spiked his bare skin. He climbed until the trunk thinned. He climbed until he passed through a blanket of fog, through the very clouds.

When he came out the other side, the branches, though still sickly, were not as black. A bit more green sprouted here and there.

The air felt cooler. The trunk was now so thin that it began to sway. This startled Pino, but he still couldn't see beyond the other treetops around him. He climbed. The trunk swayed violently. He climbed, sweat trickling into his eyes. He climbed, clenching each branch so hard his hands turned white, until finally he reached as high as he could go.

Blinking away the sweat from his eyes, trying to remain as still as possible so the tree wouldn't sway, he swept his gaze across the treetops. At last he was high enough. This tree might not be the tallest in the forest, but it was higher than most. The trees that poked up through the clouds were few and far between; they looked like birthday candles on a white cake.

Pino could not see the lake, but he *could* see a hazy purple mountain range far off in the distance, stretching as far as the eye could see. He knew those mountains. His papa had spoken of them. They were the mountains that bordered the western shore of their country.

If that was west, then Pino knew which way was north. He peered over the frothy white broth and didn't see anything that distinguished north, but regardless, that was the direction he needed to go.

He just had to keep it firmly in his mind as he crawled down the tree.

Going down seemed to take much longer. A few times he slipped and nearly plummeted, which made him even more cautious.

When he passed through the fog and had a good view of the ground, he picked out a stone just north of the tree as a marker. When he got down, he would walk toward that stone. And he would try to keep walking in that general direction.

Nearly to the bottom, it suddenly occurred to Pino that he was going about this wrong. Why walk at all? He'd brought one tree to life; why couldn't he bring another? Since he had this special gift, he might as well use it to make life easier for himself.

Perched on one of the lower branches, he pressed his palms flat against the bark. *Come alive,* he told the tree.

Nothing happened.

"Come alive," he said aloud.

Still nothing. He tried again and again, his voice getting louder and more frantic. He tried with his eyes open. He tried with his eyes closed. He concentrated, his forehead furrowing, the veins on his temples pulsing. He imagined it. He willed it. He wished for it as hard as he'd ever wished for anything in his life.

And yet, nothing.

Howling with rage, Pino climbed the rest of the way down. What good was a gift if it wasn't available to you when you needed it? He jumped to the ground and started for the stone he'd picked out above, walking first, then running. When he reached the stone, he picked another not far away, hoping he was keeping a straight line. Running faster. Not letting himself rest. If he couldn't ride a tree, he had to run as fast as his legs would carry him.

As he ran, another thought occurred to him, one that quickly dissolved his anger at not being able to use his gift and replaced it with fear.

If he couldn't use his gift, what would happen to him if the wolves came again?

There is something that happens to the human body when it is pushed past the point of exhaustion. There is something that happens when every ounce of strength is spent; when every breath burns in the lungs and every muscle throbs in agony; when every swelling joint and every quivering tendon screams in protest. There is something that happens when the saliva in the mouth tastes like acid and the heart pounding in the ears drowns out all other sounds.

Eventually all feeling goes away, all sensation departs, and the mind disengages from the enormity of the pain the body is sending its way.

That is the place where Pino went as he dashed through the dark forest—a timeless place unmoored from his surroundings, disconnected from the here and now, where the rotting trees and the uneven ground were a passing blur. He was vaguely aware that he was running—north, heading north—but it was like someone telling him a story. Even his worry was gone. He was somewhere else.

He was somewhere at peace.

That was the most amazing thing. For the first time in Pino's life, he was not filled with self-doubt. He did not feel that creeping anxiety that came from being different. He was not tormented by the relentless desire to be just like others, to not stand out in any way. He did not think about those awkward times when he got to play with other children, when he never knew quite what to say or how to say it.

It was hard to be like other children when you weren't born the same way they were born, when you were once made of wood instead of flesh.

In any case, he thought of none of that now.

Right now, he just ran.

In such a state of mind time had no meaning. It could have been minutes or hours, and the only sign that time had passed at all were the trees. Pino was so in a trance that it took him a while before he noticed that they looked healthier.

Gone were the black and withered things, the scorched bark and the branches that turned to ash at the merest touch. In their place were towering pines with reddish bark, trees that would have been impossible to climb because they bore no lower branches at all. Their trunks were as wide around as houses. Their limbs, high above, were a deep, rich green.

The sky peeking through the gaps was no longer gray; it was crimson melting into lavender. Though the light was fading, the fog had dissipated, and so the way ahead actually seemed brighter than before—a dusky light, to be sure, but still easier to see.

Healthy ferns sprang up where rotting ones had been. Leafy vines sprouted between beds of pine needles. Even the smell was different—the moist air full of life.

Pino thought the first tall trees were the biggest he'd ever seen, but then they got taller still. Mountains of wood. They weren't trees at all. They were like gods. Birds—he heard chirping, something missing before. Gray squirrels scampered out of his way, diving into a thick tangle of ivy. There was even a butterfly—a butterfly, of all things!—fluttering its yellow wings from one blooming white flower to another.

He'd gone from some of the blackest woods to some of the most beautiful in the blink of an eye.

But where was Sapphire Lake?

He'd no more thought this than he passed over a small rise—and saw a hint of blue ahead, peeking at him between the massive trees. Even from a great distance it was an incredibly vibrant shade of blue; as he drew nearer, it only became more so.

When he finally reached its shore, standing in the tall grass lining its banks, it didn't seem like a lake at all. It seemed like a bit of sky had fallen to Earth.

Hands on his knees, gasping for breath, Pino stood there on the soft bed of grass and absorbed the beauty of the lake. A pair of swans darted from the reeds and swam along the shore, their passing barely ruffling the water.

Papa.

The thought of his papa, still alone and dying in that cave, broke his reverie. Now he needed to find this girl with no arms and no legs. Where would such a girl be? Scanning the shore, he saw not a single living soul, and the thought of searching the perimeter—miles around—drained Pino of what little strength he had left. His legs, still burning, shuddered. He did not even know how much longer he could stand.

"Hey!" he cried.

It might not be the smartest thing to do—maybe the wolves were in this place too, or other hungry predators—but he was desperate.

"Hey!" he shouted again. "Anyone out there? Anyone at all?"

There was no reply. When he'd summoned his breath, he tried again. He went on shouting until his voice failed him, until his throat grew hoarse. Knowing his papa was counting on him, he tried to shake it off and shout anyway, but then his body had finally had enough.

His knees buckled. His legs gave way. He crumpled into the grass, his head and shoulders draped over the bank, one outstretched hand just touching the surface of the water. He expected the water to be cool, but it wasn't. It was warm.

When the ripples created by his touch had stilled, he saw only his reflection staring back at him—his scratched and bruised face, the red cuts and welts mixed with the layers of dirt and sweat caked on his cheeks. With the dark circles under the eyes, and the skin drawn tight against a gaunt face, it did not even look like the face of a boy.

He was looking at that face when he heard a rustle in the grass.

Seized with panic, thinking the wolves had followed him, he scrambled to his knees and spun to face them. But it wasn't wolves who'd emerged from the forest.

It was people.

There were at least a dozen of them, men and women alike, tall and slender, all but a few of them with spiky blond hair and eyes as blue as the lake, their pale, freckled skin camouflaged behind clothes fashioned out of their surroundings. Their vests and pants had been woven from the grass. Their body armor—for that's what the plates strapped to their arms, legs, and chests looked like to Pino—had been constructed using the reddish bark from the giant trees.

Even their crossbows were made of the same stuff, making them nearly impossible to see unless they moved them.

Which they were doing.

Raising them up.

Pointing them at Pino.

Fingers tightening on the triggers.

CHAPTER NINE

These people of the woods, they did not have kind faces. Their faces were like their polished granite arrowheads—hard, cruel, and razor sharp. The man in the front had the hardest face of all. He was the oldest of the bunch, his hair more white than blond, his cheekbones so sharp Pino could have pricked his fingers on them. His skin was weathered and bleached. On his left cheek he bore a small scar shaped like a crescent moon.

"You're trespassing on sacred land," he said, lowering his crossbow slightly. "The penalty is death."

"But—but I didn't know—," Pino protested.

"Ignorance is no excuse."

"Wait!"

The man again raised his crossbow. Pino thought about diving into the lake, but he knew the arrows would strike him before he even touched the water. He couldn't believe the voice in the cave had sent him to the lake only to have him die.

"I'm here to see the girl with no arms and no legs!" he cried.

With his voice still ringing in the open air, Pino closed his eyes and clenched his teeth. He was sure the arrows were going to fly. A few seconds passed, the breeze humming over the water and whispering through the grass.

"What did you say?" the man asked.

Pino swallowed, cracking open his eyes. The woods people were still pointing their crossbows, but now their faces looked more confused than angry. "I said I'm here to see the girl with no arms and no legs," he repeated.

"How do you know her?" the man demanded. "Who are you? What do you want?"

Pino told them his name and why he'd come. He said he'd been told she could save his papa, who was right this minute dying in a cave, and at this they murmured and exchanged glances.

"Do you know where she is?" he asked hopefully.

Finally the man in front lowered his crossbow. The others quickly followed suit.

"Of course we do," he said. "You speak of Elendrew, the one with special sight. She is our queen."

With the blindfold over his eyes, Pino couldn't see a single thing. They hadn't walked long, an hour at most, but he'd already lost his sense of direction. He heard a growing chorus of crickets. He heard water murmuring over polished rocks. He heard the whispers of the woodsfolk, all of whom kept their voices too low for him to make out what they were saying.

Worrying about his papa, he was about to ask how much farther it was when the crunch of pine needles on soft earth changed to the dull thudding of wooden planks. He heard a creak and a thud, like a gate shutting, then someone took his hand and placed it on rough rope.

"Hold this," a woman instructed.

Before he could ask why, the planks beneath him shuddered, and he grabbed the rope for balance. He heard a rhythmic ticking, like someone banging two sticks together. His stomach dropped suddenly, as if they were moving upward. How could that be?

The ticking went on for some minutes, until the planks shuddered, then fell still. Finally his blindfold was removed.

The sensation of rising had been a correct one; they were high up in the giant trees, so high that when Pino peered over the rope that acted as a rail on the wooden platform where he stood, he could not see the forest floor. It was lost in the labyrinth of leafy green branches and foliage below.

Of all the stories his papa used to tell him at night, none could prepare him for the awesome sight of the city in the trees. At most it might have been only thirty or forty dwellings, each of them no bigger than the cottage Pino and Geppetto used to call home, but what other word could describe such a splendidly constructed place?

Not a village. Not a town. It was a city, all right, a city of rope bridges and thatched roofs, a city of houses half carved into the thick trunks and half built outside them—but so expertly made, with the same bark and pine needles that made up the tree itself, that only the tendrils of smoke rising from their chimneys and the yellow glow from their windows grabbed his attention. Otherwise, his eye would have skipped right past them.

In all his wildest dreams he could not have imagined such a place.

They'd ridden up on some kind of platform, one attached by thick gray ropes to a series of spoked wheels. He was prodded off the platform onto a much bigger platform, one that circled the trunk of a massive tree, a dozen rope bridges leading to the houses around it. The people filed onto the platform, dispersing onto the various bridges. People emerged from the tree houses, people clad in the same woven clothes but not the wooden armor, and waved at them. Even some children. They seemed happy.

Pino marveled at it all, still not quite believing his eyes. "Why did I have to be blindfolded," he asked, "if you're letting me see it now?"

The man with the scar on his cheek smirked. "Because you cannot see our home from the ground," he said. "Come now, Queen Elendrew does not like to be kept waiting."

"I don't want to wait either," Pino said, thinking of his papa. "What's your name?"

The man pointed at the bridge nearest to them, one that led to what appeared to be the tiniest house of all. "My name's Olan," he said, "but I'd save your questions for her. There's no point in telling you more if she doesn't believe your story."

His warning sounded ominous. "What do you mean?" Pino asked.

"I mean, if she doesn't believe you, your stay here will be too short to bother with names. And I must also tell you that it's a long way down for departed guests, especially those who don't get to ride our ropefloat."

Starting up the rope bridge, feeling the planks sway gently beneath him, Pino didn't even want to think about falling from such a height.

CHAPTER TEN

The little house at the end of the rope bridge was deceiving to the eye. From the outside it hardly looked big enough to contain a single person, just a simple green door with a pine needle roof, but inside was a very different story.

Inside it was as big as a cathedral.

From the looks of it, most of the trunk of the big tree had been hollowed out, polished smooth, and stained a warm golden hue. The ceiling narrowed to a point high above, higher than any church steeple. He saw a ring of tiny oval openings up there that had been invisible from the outside. Flickering lanterns, low to the floor, encircled the area, leaving the ceiling shrouded in darkness.

Ahead of them, in the middle of the great room, a woman sat on a throne that seemed to rise directly out of the floor— carved from the tree itself, Pino thought. Behind the throne was a dwelling all its own, one Pino had not seen at first because it was made of glass, so clear it was as if the walls weren't even there. He saw a bed of straw in the glass house. He saw a chair, dressers, cabinets.

Around the woman on the throne dozens of the woodsfolk knelt on blankets made of woven grass, silent and unmoving. The woman herself was just as still.

Or not a woman—a girl, at the tail end of her youth. Olan guided Pino to her, another three men in their wake, and as they approached, Pino got a better look at her in the light from the flickering torches on either side of her. She might have been anywhere from thirteen to nineteen; it was hard to tell because she had such a stern face, and because her billowing white gown made it hard to see her figure.

Yet Pino could see her arms and legs. She definitely had them: slender fingers resting on the arms of the throne, narrow feet in slippers made of white rose petals.

It was an odd thing to be disappointed that someone had arms and legs, but that's how Pino felt. He had no idea why the man with the scar thought this girl, this Elendrew, was the same person he needed to find.

All of this effort was for nothing.

She did not look like the other woodsfolk. Her hair was long and black, her skin a deep reddish brown, similar to the bark of the trees they called home. Where the woodsfolk were tall and slender, she was shorter and a bit broader. Where they had blue eyes, hers were as black as charred wood.

They had not even stopped walking when she said, "Tell me why you are here, boy."

Her voice carried up into the shadows. The way she said the words, it was like she was used to being obeyed.

When Pino told her his name, and that he'd come because his papa was dying, she just went on staring at him.

"And why do you think I can help?" she asked.

"I don't know if you can," Pino said. "I need to find a girl with no arms and no legs."

She laughed—a horrible sound, as sharp as a dagger and

just as cutting. "Well, you've come to the right place. I am Elendrew, and I am the one you seek. Now tell me, who is it that told you I would be here?"

Pino didn't understand. "But your arms and legs—," he began.

"Are completely useless," she finished, grimacing. "Haven't you noticed how still I am? How I have not moved my hands even so much as a twitch? It's not because I don't want to move. It's because I *can't.*"

"Oh," Pino said.

"Don't look so *relieved,*" Elendrew said. "I was born with this curse. Now, what's wrong with your hand?"

"What?" The question caught Pino by surprise.

"Your right hand," she said. "Look at it. The first finger— the skin looks funny."

When Pino held up his right hand, he was alarmed to see that she was right. The very tip of his first finger was . . . different. Instead of pink, it was brown, like a strange callus. But when he rubbed the skin with his thumb, it wasn't a callus at all. In fact, it wasn't even skin.

It was wood.

There was no doubt it would have been easy to give in to the panic swelling inside him, but Pino didn't have time for panic right now. He had to focus on his papa. "I don't know," he said, trying to keep the nervousness out of his voice. "I think—I think I burned it back in the fire."

From how far away she was, Pino didn't think she could see his finger well enough to know he was lying, but she still stared a long time before replying.

"A funny-looking burn," she said. "But enough of that for now. Who told you I could help your papa?"

"She didn't have a name," Pino said.

"What? What nonsense is this?"

"She was just a voice—a voice in a cave."

This changed everything. Her icy gaze turned to astonishment. It wasn't just Elendrew gaping at him either—everyone in the room, those who had brought him to her, those praying on the floor, all of them stared openly at him. It was so quiet he heard the torches hissing like angry serpents.

"What did you say?" she asked.

The severity of her gaze, the sheer intensity of it, made Pino queasy. He swallowed away the lump in his throat. "I said, she was just a—"

"Yes, yes, I heard you," she snapped. "Where is this cave? How did you come to find it? Tell me exactly."

Slowly, haltingly, Pino told her as best he could about his journey since they'd left home. He didn't tell her why they'd fled—nothing about Antoinette, or about how he'd brought her to life—but he told her about their escape from the giant wolves with the red eyes, about how they took refuge in the cave, where he spoke to a voice that danced in blue light.

"I know this cave," Elendrew said.

"You do?"

"Yes. I was there too, as a very small child. It's where my mother left me." Her voice became dreamy, her eyes distant. "Why, you may wonder? I was very young, but I remember how she looked at me. How she could barely *stand* to look at me. My arms and legs may have looked fine, but they might as well have been missing, for all the good they did. She left me there to die, I imagine, but I heard the voice too. It told me it spoke only to people who were special. It told me if I just stayed calm, someone would come. And so they did. These people, they call themselves the People of the Tall Trees—they came for me, and I have been here ever since. Because I have a way of knowing things that others can't know, a way of seeing things no one else can see, they made me their queen."

Pino had never had a mother, but he imagined that it would be even worse to *have* a mother only to have her abandon you. He felt sorry for Elendrew, but he didn't know what to say and he didn't have time to think of something. "My papa—," he began.

"Yes, yes," Elendrew said, "we all know of your papa. Tell me, Pino, why are you special?"

"What?"

"The voice in the cave—she speaks only to those who are special. So what makes you special, Pino?"

Pino hesitated. He didn't know why, but something told him he should not tell her about Antoinette or about how he'd brought the tree to life. But he needed to tell her something. If he lied completely, she would see right through him as if he were made of glass like the dwelling behind her.

"I was once made out of wood," he said.

Her eyebrows arched. "Oh. Well, that is indeed something special. You were made out of wood and you became real?"

He nodded.

"How?"

"I don't know."

"A pity. Perhaps that knowledge would be useful. If it's one thing we have in abundance, it's wood." She sighed. "Well, unless you have something more important to say, Olan will show you to a room—"

"My papa, my papa!" Pino cried. "Please, he's dying back in that cave. Can't you do something to help?"

"Oh yes," Elendrew said. "Your precious papa. Well, it is true that we *could* help him. One of my many talents is that I am skilled in the ways of healing."

"Oh good!"

"Yes. But now you must tell me why I *should*."

"What?"

Elendrew frowned. "Nothing is free in this world, boy. Everything comes with a cost. If you want me to do something for *you*, you must do something for *me*."

"But I don't have any money! I don't have anything! I—I don't even have a shirt!"

Her dark eyes narrowed. "It doesn't have to be something you could give me. It could be something you could do. Think hard. There must be something. It can't be something my people can do for me either, because they attend to my every need. It must be something *special*."

Pino felt all of the eyes of the people in the room boring into him. Somewhere far away his papa was alone in the dark, each breath perhaps his last. What a terrible thing. What a terrible, awful, horrible thing to be standing among all these people who could help and yet were unwilling to do so just out of the goodness of their hearts. Pino did not understand it. If he were them, he would gladly help someone in need without payment of any kind.

But maybe he was wrong.

Maybe that's not the way the world worked. Maybe he needed to be more careful about who he helped and why. After all, hadn't Papa refused to help all those people who'd come to him for help, all those people who'd lost someone they loved?

Pino knew that was different, though. He knew Papa

hadn't helped those people because he didn't think he could. Papa had thought making those puppets would only make them more sad, and after what happened with Antoinette, Pino had to agree. Some kinds of help weren't really help at all. These woods people, they could help in a real way and they just didn't want to try. Pino didn't want to be like them.

He looked at Elendrew. What could he do for her? The only thing she really needed was new arms and new legs—and then the idea came to him. He looked at the wooden plates his escorts wore on their arms and legs.

Could it be so simple?

"What is it?" Elendrew asked. "Have you thought of something?"

"I think so," Pino said. "I think—yes, I think I could make you new arms and legs."

"What?"

"Well, not *exactly* new arms and legs. But some you can use."

She frowned, the lines on her face deepening. "Boy, you better explain yourself before—"

"I can make you a wooden suit," Pino said quickly.

When she still looked confused, he explained his idea. Had she heard of the suits of armor that men in the old days wore? Instead of metal, Pino would make her a suit of wood. It would fit her as snugly as a second skin. When she wore it, she would be able to walk about and grab things just like everyone else.

Elendrew looked skeptical. "Why would wearing a wooden suit allow me to do that?"

"Because," Pino said, knowing he couldn't avoid coming out with the truth any longer, "I could make it do so. I—I have that gift. The ability to bring wood to life." There was something quite different in Elendrew's eyes now.

The skepticism had been replaced by a desperate hope. Her eyes brimmed with tears.

"You could do this?" she said.

He nodded. "If you save my papa."

"Hmm. Well, then. I suppose we better get to it."

Quickly she gave instructions to the men who'd brought Pino to seek out the cave and find Pino's papa. She told them that it was vital they hurry, that they should bring him straight to her, along with all of her herbs and extracts. She told them to take a dozen people and not rest for even a moment.

When the men had gone, she again looked at Pino, and there was something chilling in her gaze.

CHAPTER ELEVEN

The woodsfolk brought Pino all the tools and supplies he needed to fashion Elendrew her wooden suit, but he had a hard time concentrating until the men finally arrived with his papa—unconscious and prone on a litter made of thick vines, but still breathing. It was a faint breath, barely felt even when Pino leaned his ear next to his papa's bluish lips, but it was there.

He was still alive, not by much, perhaps, but Elendrew said a little alive was all that mattered.

The healing was all done in the great chamber. After some women had tended to Geppetto's wounds—cleaning them with steaming water, applying a salve that looked and smelled like warm mud, then affixing bandages made from large, leafy ferns—he was spoon-fed a bubbling broth that Elendrew herself had created.

Well, not her exactly, of course, since she couldn't add the ingredients or do the mixing herself, but she had personally overseen its creation. She told her attendants the specific roots and spices she wanted in the cauldron. She told them exactly how long it was to boil, and how much to give him when it was done.

The green sludge looked awful, like something scooped

out of a pond, but it smelled as sweet as chocolate.

When she finished with Geppetto, he was hauled away on the litter to gain his strength in another place. Standing behind the workbench filled with all the wood and all the stone tools he'd asked for, Pino watched him leave. He'd taken to keeping his right hand, with its partial wooden finger, slightly behind him so as not to raise more questions. He also didn't want to look at it himself. It scared him and he hoped it would just go away.

"But I want to be with him," Pino insisted.

"Oh, no," Elendrew said. "He needs peace and quiet, and the sounds of you working would not help at all. You *do* want him to get better, don't you?"

Pino nodded.

"Well, then," she went on, "he'll need at least a week of rest before he's well enough to walk again. Besides, you have much work to do. I would not want you to be distracted. You will work and sleep here until you're done."

"It might take a while," Pino warned.

"How long?"

In the dim light of the chamber Pino surveyed the spread of wood and tools. The truth was he really didn't know how long it would take, or even if he could do it at all. He'd been Geppetto's apprentice for less than two months, and there was still much about wood carving he did not know.

He also didn't know if he'd be able to bring it to life as he'd promised. He remembered his failure the second time he'd tried to bring a tree to life.

What he really needed was a chance to escape before she realized he couldn't do as he'd promised, but he needed Geppetto to be better first. If he couldn't even walk, they wouldn't get far.

"Maybe a week," he said, thinking how long Elendrew had said it would take for his papa to heal.

She shook her head. "You have five days. You better work quickly."

Working quickly was the one thing Pino *didn't* want to do. Much as when he made the puppet of Antoinette, Pino found that working with wood came naturally. The tools they'd brought him weren't at all like the ones he'd used back home—these were made mostly of stone and glass—but he took to them just the same. In fact, the work was going so well that he had to force himself to go slower.

If he finished the suit in a day or two, it was doubtful his papa would be well enough to travel.

And Pino also needed time to plan his escape.

Unfortunately, since he worked right beside Elendrew, it was difficult to work *too* slowly. Food was brought to him when needed—delicious food, tender bird meat glazed with honey, fruit so succulent it burst with juice when he bit into it, and a kind of bread that was so soft it dissolved in his mouth and tasted like cake. He would have tried to stretch out the meals, but the food was so good, and he was so famished from working, that he couldn't stop himself from devouring it.

All the while Pino studied Elendrew. He watched the way her attendants tended to her needs—feeding her, adjusting her in her chair when she complained of being sore, even carrying her off to the toilet room at the back of the chamber when she said she needed to relieve herself. At first Pino felt sorry for her, not being able to do any of these simple things herself, but this feeling didn't last too long. Soon he watched her more with awe than pity.

Three or four times every hour someone came to her asking her to make a decision—sometimes big ones, sometimes small ones, but always she had an answer. Where should they hunt for deer today? "Try the east side of the lake," she would tell them. What should a mother do about a daughter who couldn't sleep? A certain herbal remedy was suggested. With winter coming on, were there any special preparations they should make? Yes, this year they needed as much Gaslin root as they could find, for there was going to be an awful virus that would sweep through the people.

She always had an answer. It was like she just knew things. Important things. It truly was a special gift.

Carving one of the arm joints, wood chips flying, Pino began to wonder what it would be like to be her—to be so smart, and to have every need fulfilled. Maybe having arms and legs that didn't work would be a small price to pay for such a life. Someone was always watching her, so she knew that no harm would come her way. Even when she slept, she slept in a glass house so that the people outside—for there were always people praying outside, it seemed—could see if there was anything wrong.

Mostly, though, Pino worked. His hands became cramped from gripping the tools for so many hours. Wood dust clouded his eyes. At night he slept in a cot behind his workbench. When he ate, he ate there as well. After a while he complained about not getting any fresh air, and Elendrew permitted him to take a couple breaks each day outside, but only for five minutes at a time.

Pino was on one of these breaks, standing in the middle of one of the rope bridges in the foggy morning air, when a girl about his age came bounding toward him. He'd been staring at his wooden fingertip—the stupid thing still hadn't gone back to normal—and he whipped it behind his back at her approach.

The girl was riding a fake wolf, one made out of wood, with a carved wolf head and a pole for a body. Each time she bounded, the whole bridge shook. Her hair, nearly white, seemed to glow in the fog. The moisture in the air glistened on her dimpled cheeks. She stared at him so intently that Pino became uncomfortable and looked over the rope rail. Somewhere far below, a bird darted through the fog. It was the only bird he'd seen in all the time he'd been standing there. He figured birds just didn't fly that high.

"You're Pino," she said.

"That's right," he said warily. He fidgeted with the sleeves of his shirt, the same one he'd given to Papa to stop his bleeding. The woodsfolk had cleaned it, and now it was as good as new.

"I'm Aki," she said.

"Hello."

She stepped off of her pretend wolf and leaned on the rope railing. "I heard you was once made of wood," she said.

"Um, yes," Pino said. "That's right."

"Were you a table?"

"No."

"Were you a chair?"

"No."

"Well, what were you, then? Were you a tree? If you were a tree, you must not have been a very big tree. A little sapling, I think."

"I wasn't a tree. Or maybe I was once. I don't remember. I was a puppet."

She giggled. "That's so strange. I have a puppet. Lots of kids here have puppets. Her name is Kelty. Did you have strings? Did people make you dance? I can make Kelty dance."

Pino shrugged. "I don't know. I don't remember much from then. It's all kind of foggy."

"Do you have strings now?"

"No, no. I'm a real boy."

"How did you become a real boy?"

"Um, well, I just wished for it."

"You just wished for it and it came true?"

"Yes. Eventually."

She sighed. "I wish for lots of things and they don't come true. Yesterday I wished to be an eagle. I wished and I wished so I could fly high in the clouds and look down on everything so small. But it didn't happen."

"I'm sorry," he said.

She shrugged. "I'm used to it. Like how I wished for Mother to come back. But she didn't. That didn't happen either."

"Oh. Where did she go?"

She grew thoughtful, her glistening forehead wrinkling. "Well . . . Father told me she went on a trip. A very long trip. But I know that's not true. I know she died last winter when lots of people got sick. Father just says she went on a trip so he's not sad. And that's okay. I don't tell him the truth because I don't want him to be sad. It's no fun being sad. Are you sad sometimes, Pino?"

"Sometimes," Pino said, nodding.

"I think it's normal to be sad."

"I think so," Pino agreed, though he still wasn't sure what was normal. He wished he hadn't been forced to tell them all about his past. Now, no matter what he did, they would always treat him differently. He would always be the boy who was once a puppet.

He vowed that if he ever ended up in another place where people didn't know him, where he could start fresh, he would keep his past a secret.

Knowing Elendrew would be irritated if he delayed any longer, he turned to head back inside—then realized that he might be able to learn something from this girl to help him escape.

"Aki?" he said.

She smiled. "I like it when you say my name."

"Oh. Um, can I ask you something?"

"Green," she said.

"What?"

"I thought you wanted to ask me what my favorite color is," she explained. "It's green. I know that's not very interesting. That's what lots of kids say, because green is so pretty here."

"It is," he agreed. "No, I want to ask you, um, well—is the ropefloat the only way down?"

"Why? Do you want to go down?"

"No, no, I was just curious."

"It would take a long time to go down."

"I don't want to go down. I just—"

"I could ask Father to take us down. It would be fun. We could go exploring and have a picnic."

"No!"

Pino hadn't meant to yell, but Aki was getting so carried away that he was afraid it wouldn't be long before she was marching straight in to Elendrew to announce that Pino would be going down to the forest floor. The little girl looked quite taken aback, blinking rapidly, a flush in her cheeks.

"Well, you don't need to *shout*," she said.

"I'm sorry."

"I'm standing right here, after all."

"I know."

"If you don't want to go, it's not really a big deal. I can always go with someone *else*."

"Yes. That's true. I was just—I was curious about getting down, that's all."

"Well, *of course* everybody knows the ropefloat is the only way down."

"Oh." Pino's heart sank. If he needed to escape without being seen, it would be hard to do it when there was only one way down. Everybody would be looking in the same place.

"Except in an emergency," she added.

"What?"

She sighed, drumming her fingers on the rope railing. "We practice it all the time. After you're here a little while, you'll practice it too."

"What do you mean?"

"The featherwings, silly! What do you think I mean? After the great shaking a few years ago, when some of the tall trees fell, Elendrew ordered us all to make featherwings. They're not wings, really, that's just what we call them. If they were real wings, maybe we could fly and I wouldn't have to wish for it anymore. These just kind of let you float gently to the ground. So in case the ropefloat isn't working, like if it was broken during a great shaking, then we could get down."

"Where do you keep them?"

She shot him a look. "You can't use them *now*!"

"I know, I know! I was just curious."

"Well, we keep them under our beds, of course. Everybody does. Where else should we keep them?"

"Oh."

She shook her head. "Pino, you really don't know very much, do you?"

"No," he said with a great sigh of his own, "I guess I don't."

CHAPTER TWELVE

F ive days later not only was the wooden suit finished, but Pino also had his plan of escape.

It was a simple plan, but it required everything to go exactly right. When he showed Elendrew the finished wooden suit, he told her that in order for it to be brought to life, his papa would have to be present. He'd always brought wood to life with Papa in the room, he insisted, and he didn't think he could do it any other way. He also told her that it couldn't be done inside her chamber. It had to be done in the open air, because wood did not want to be brought to life inside other wood.

If Elendrew was suspicious, she didn't show it. If anything, she looked giddy with anticipation.

She ordered that Geppetto be brought to the Great Platform, what they called the central area with the ropefloat. She told Pino that all of the People of the Tall Trees would gather on the platform and the adjoining bridges to witness her putting on the suit for the first time.

"It will be a momentous occasion," she said, "and I want to share it with everyone."

Pino's plan was to create some kind of distraction so that he and Geppetto could flee into one of the dwellings, find a pair of featherwings, then escape to the ground. It needed to go exactly right or someone would just grab them and prevent them from leaving.

It rained heavily that morning, a crackling downpour on the leafy branches, but it was over within an hour, and the sun was doing its best to pierce the trees. By the time the woodsfolk began to gather on the platform around noon, it was unusually warm for a fall day, and the air smelled heavy and rich with living things.

When they saw his suit, people began to murmur excitedly. It wasn't perfect by any means, but it was still a far cry from anything even the most experienced wood-carver could create.

Rather than being big and bulky like a suit of armor, his wooden suit would fit her more like a second skin, painted white with red trimmings, the joints that connected the arms and legs mostly hidden behind decorative white lace. From far away it wouldn't even look like a wooden suit; it would look more like some courtly outfit, especially when he added the final piece: a flowing red gown woven directly into the suit's shoulders.

Standing there next to his creation, people milling about and admiring it, Pino had one problem.

He'd begun to have second thoughts about leaving.

After five days of living among the People of the Tall Trees, he still didn't quite feel like one of them, but he thought he *might* feel like one of them eventually. On each of his breaks he had watched the woodsfolk going about their lives: women carting water up from the trickling springs below; children laughing and playing with balls and stones; men returning from a hunt with rousing tales of their exploits.

They seemed like such a happy people. He really did want to stay.

Unfortunately, he had no confidence that he would be able to bring the suit to life. Of course he *hoped* the suit would come to life—it would make things much easier—but he wasn't counting on it. And if he failed, then Elendrew was going to toss both him and Geppetto over the side. Better to make a run for it at the first opportunity.

When everyone's attention was focused on her, that's when they would make their move.

Still, watching everyone's smiling, excited faces in the warm glow from the brightening sun, Pino hated to think about leaving. It didn't help at all when Aki showed up on the platform. She wore a pretty yellow dress made from daffodil petals.

She beamed at him and took his hand. He smiled back. So this was how it felt to have a friend.

"What's wrong with your hand?" she asked.

"Huh? Oh, that." He pulled his hand away and thrust it behind him. He'd been concentrating so hard on finishing the wooden suit that he hadn't given it much thought, even though it clearly wasn't getting better. "It's just, um, sore—you know, from all the working."

"It felt like wood."

"Yeah, sometimes it gets like that."

"Hello, son," said a man from behind.

The voice was so gruff and hoarse that at first Pino didn't recognize it—but then he knew who it was. Spinning around, he saw his beloved papa leaning on a gnarled cane, his curly white hair framing his gaunt face. He was almost as thin as Pino, and his knees trembled as if he might topple at any moment. But he was alive. Alive and smiling. They'd even mended his clothes—the white shirt and brown pants looked nearly as good as new.

Words failing him, Pino wrapped his arms around Geppetto and squeezed as tight as he could.

Geppetto let out a grunt of air. "*Ooof.* Careful, son, I'm not all that steady on my feet yet."

"They wouldn't let me see you, Papa! They wouldn't let me!"

Geppetto patted Pino's head. "I know. It's all right. I was sleeping most of the time anyway."

There was so much more that Pino wanted to say, but then a hush fell over the crowd. All the heads turned and looked in the same direction—toward Elendrew's dwelling. Pino looked as well and saw the procession approaching along the rope bridge, two women in the back, two in the front, and Elendrew sitting upon her ornately carved oak chair in the center.

Instead of her enormous, stately gown, she wore a simple white dress, one that made her look more like the child she was than a regal queen. She rode with a solemn expression, but her eyes gleamed.

The leftover rain, dripping from the wet leaves, glittered like diamonds in the shafts of sunlight. The village was so still that when the water plinked on the wooden planks, it could be heard by all.

"Are you ready, boy?" Elendrew asked.

When all eyes turned next to him, Pino found he couldn't speak. His throat had seized up on him again.

"Ready for what?" Geppetto said.

"We've made a bargain, old man," Elendrew said. "Your life for this wooden suit—one that will allow me to walk again."

Geppetto began to protest, but Pino grabbed his arm. "It's all right, Papa," he said, finally managing to squeeze out some words.

"But Pino—"

"It's ready!" Pino announced to Elendrew. He felt Geppetto's angry glare on his face, but he couldn't worry about that now. There was no time to explain the plan. "Put it on and I'll—I'll give it life."

Everyone watched as Elendrew's attendants maneuvered her into the suit, working her arms and legs as if she were some kind of doll. If she'd had strings, she would have made a good puppet, Pino thought, and then felt bad for thinking it.

As Elendrew's attendants finished putting on the suit, tightening the clasps that held the pieces together, Pino took Geppetto's hand and led him through the throng of people. When he resisted at first, Pino gave him a serious look, and Geppetto reluctantly went along.

"Where are you going?" Aki asked.

"Just need to, um, get a little better view," Pino explained.

"I'll go with you," she said.

He wanted to tell her that probably wasn't such a good idea, but since other woodsfolk had overheard their conversation and were watching them, he couldn't very well do that. Together they wove through the people and started up one of the bridges—not going too far, of course, but far enough that there were only a handful of woodsfolk, mostly children, between them and the dwelling at the end of the rope bridge.

Close enough that when the time came, they could make a dash for the featherwings that were inside.

The thought of jumping into the swirling mists, not being able to see the ground far below, made Pino feel queasy, but he was going to do it.

When Elendrew was ready, Pino raised his voice so all could hear.

"This is very important," he said. "I need everyone to close their eyes. I want you to close your eyes and wish very hard that you want Elendrew's suit to come to life. It really does help. The more people that wish, the easier it is for me."

There was murmuring. People exchanged glances.

"Go on now," Pino said. "If you don't do it, it may not work. Do you want that?"

There was more murmuring, and then people began to close their eyes—all but Elendrew. She stared at him in a very strange way, her eyes wide and quivering.

"You especially, Elendrew," Pino said to her. "I need you to close your eyes and wish for it very, very hard."

She nodded and, with a trembling lip, closed her eyes. Now was their chance. They had to be swift. Pino took Geppetto by the elbow and pushed him up the rope bridge. His papa's eyes fluttered open, but Pino put a finger to his lips.

If Pino had gone right then without looking back, perhaps the plan would have worked exactly as he'd intended. Perhaps they would have gotten to those featherwings and escaped, leaving Elendrew and the People of the Tall Trees behind without ever having to deal with them again.

But Pino *did* look back. He looked back and saw something quite startling that stopped him in his tracks.

A tear rolled down Elendrew's cheek.

It was the first of many. Her eyes were still closed, the eyelids trembling, as other tears formed tracks down her skin. Watching these tears, Pino felt his heart go out to Elendrew in a way that it hadn't before.

He knew what that strange look on her face was about now. The same look must have been on Pino's face not that many months ago, when he stood before the glimmering turquoise fairy as a clunky wooden copy of a boy—hoping, wishing, *praying* that she could transform him into a real boy.

What if the fairy had done as Pino was doing, and turned her back on him?

If that was all Pino had seen, he might still have gone—after all, his love for his papa outweighed his sympathy for Elendrew—but he also saw another thing. He also saw Aki, who was now staring at him with her eyes open. He could see that she knew what he'd been planning, and the disappointment on her face was all the proof he needed that what he was doing was wrong.

He could not leave Elendrew this way.

With a sigh, he started back through the throng of people. When Geppetto started after him, Pino shook his head. The creak of his footsteps on the planks turned a few heads his way, encouraging people to open their eyes. Elendrew, cheeks glistening with her tears, also looked at him.

"Well?" she said. "Have you failed me?"

"There's one more thing," Pino said.

The entire village watched him approach. Pino did not know if his touch was required to make his gift work, but it seemed like it was, and he couldn't afford to get this one wrong. Elendrew's gaze was already melting from hope to suspicion. To make it look impressive, he knelt before her, pressing both hands against the white wooden plates covering her shins. The paint still felt slightly tacky.

Now it was Pino who had his eyes closed, and he was the only one. He focused all his desire on bringing the wooden suit to life. He did not wish for it because he wanted to escape. He wished for it because he wanted Elendrew to have a better life.

He wanted her to experience things she hadn't been able to experience before—strolling through the forest, hugging someone back, eating on her own rather than being fed. He wished for it out of love. He wished for it in the same way the turquoise fairy had wished for it—as a gift for someone who needed it, as an act of kindness out of the goodness of his heart.

"My queen!"

It was Olan who spoke first, but other shouts quickly rose up from all the people. When Pino opened his eyes, he saw why.

She was standing.

Kneeling before her, his hands still on her shins, Pino felt like he was looking up at some kind of god. The way she towered over him in her glorious white suit, a suit that made her as tall and as broad as any man in the village, her red robe billowing in the breeze, the sun lancing through the trees at her back, so that she was surrounded by a golden halo—there was no way to look at her as anything but a god.

And Pino had done it. *He* had given the suit life. It was so wonderful to be able to use his gift to help someone. Now they would be able to stay with these people and call this their home.

Everyone in the village must have looked upon their queen with the same sort of awe, because they all joined Pino in kneeling before her—heads bowed, many of them crying.

"My queen, my dear queen," Olan whispered. "Now you finally have what you have long wished. Our hearts fill with joy. They fill with joy! Tell us what you need—anything your heart desires!"

Elendrew stepped forward. Her walk was jerky, much as it had been with Antoinette, but this did not seem to bother her. She still gazed at her new body with amazement. Pino, watching her closely, scooted out of the way. What would be the first thing she would want to do? Pino remembered the first thing *he* had wanted to do when he was transformed: He had wanted to hug his papa. He had wanted to tell him how much he loved him.

She raised her arms, the movement coming in starts and stops, the joints creaking. She gazed at her outstretched hands, sheathed with wooden gloves, the fingers grasping at the air. Then she turned her gaze toward Olan.

"There is only one thing my heart desires," she said. "There is only one thing, and now I can make it happen. Finally, after all these years."

She smiled a cruel smile, perhaps the cruelest smile Pino had ever seen. She waited until all the people had finally looked up at her, their faces full of confusion.

"Now," she said softly, "you will all die."

CHAPTER THIRTEEN

I t was such an unexpected thing for Elendrew to say that for a moment no one moved. Her cruel smile remained. Clouds drifted in front of the sun, darkening the forest, her red cloak deepening to a terrible shade of crimson.

Pino didn't understand. Had she misspoken?

"My queen," Olan said finally, "I'm afraid—I'm afraid you've confused us. Did you say—"

"I said I want you all to die," Elendrew said simply.

The people shuffled on their feet. There was some nervous laughter. But Pino didn't laugh. The words were spoken in the kind of evenhanded way, without malice or rage, that actually made him more afraid. He edged a little farther away, toward his papa.

"My queen—," Olan began again.

"How did you *think* I would feel?" Elendrew retorted. She took a few lumbering steps, and people backed away quickly, giving her a wide berth. "Did you think I would be *grateful*? Oh yes, I suppose that's what you would think. Because you have always been so proud of what you have done to me. You have always thought you *rescued* me. But you did not rescue me. You forced me to be something I never wanted to be."

"But, my queen," Olan protested, "if we had not brought you here—"

"Be silent!" Elendrew bellowed.

Now all the hope and love in everyone's eyes was gone, and they gazed upon the woman in the wooden suit with newfound fear.

"Think!" she cried. "Use what little brains you have! Did I ever *ask* to be made your queen? Did I ever *want* to be forced to lead your pitiful little people? No! No! *No!*"

Not a single person dared respond. Some, like Pino, crept away from her, though most simply stared, dumbfounded.

"Decisions!" she shouted, arms punching the air wildly, as if she wasn't quite in control of them. "So many decisions! Dozens of times a day you came to me asking for a decision! 'Where should we hunt, my queen?' 'How bad will the winter be, my queen?' 'What should I do about this little bee sting, my queen?' Bah! I did not want to be that person! I wanted to be left alone! To be left in peace! But would you listen to me? No!"

"But, my queen," Olan said, rising shakily, "if only you would have told—"

"I *did* tell you, old fool! How many times did I complain of being tired? How many times did I say it would be nice to have some time alone? But what did you do? You ignored me! You even made me sleep in a room with glass walls, so that I was *never* free from your incessant whining! I—never—had—one—minute's—PEACE!"

She screamed, all of her control gone, and marched around in a circle like a mad person, punching and kicking at the air as if she were fighting someone they couldn't see. Then she stopped at her wooden chair and seized it, lifting it high in the air as if it weighed nothing at all.

With one great heave she tossed the chair at Olan. He ducked out of the way, but her strength was such that the chair sailed far past him, into the open air, and then smashed into one of the rope bridges leading to the central platform—instantly smashing it into two.

There were people on that bridge, and Pino watched them scramble to either side as the two pieces of the bridge fell. Most made it to the platforms, but a few didn't, and Pino cringed, as he expected them to fall to their death. Fortunately, these woodsfolk were accustomed to living high among the trees, and they managed to twist their arms around the rope railings, saving themselves.

For a few seconds nobody moved, then chaos broke out among the people. There was a stampede. Olan, a pleading look on his face, approached Elendrew, but she hurled him away. He barely avoided plummeting off the edge, clinging on to the platform with his fingernails.

Elendrew's rage was only growing. She shrieked and she screamed. She snarled and she spit. Anyone who came at her, she flung aside. She ripped up the planks and shot them through the air. One of the planks shot through a window, smashing into a lantern, and then a fire leaped out and engulfed the dwelling. The fire swept along the bridges and jumped from one house to the next, and soon the whole city in the trees was ablaze.

Smoke choked the air. There was such a crush of bodies that Pino had a hard time finding Geppetto—just frantic people bumping up against him, their faces full of panic, and it was all he could do to keep from getting trampled. Everyone was fleeing to their dwellings, and within seconds people were diving off the rope bridges with white bundles attached to their backs.

The people didn't plummet long before their bundles opened and hundreds of whirling feathers spread behind them, slowing their descent. The opening of the chutes sounded like gunshots, but this was followed by the steady buzz of the spinning feathers. Up high the air looked like it was filled with hundreds of puffy white dandelion seeds. The featherwings swooped and banked to avoid the maze of branches.

Elendrew herself was lost in the haze of gray smoke, but her rampage continued unabated. Wooden planks shot through the air like missiles. Finally a rough hand seized Pino by the shoulder. It was Geppetto.

"Papa!" he said, coughing, waving away the smoke. "I'm so sorry! I didn't know she—"

"No time for that, son," he said. "Let's head for the ropefloat."

But they managed only a few steps in that direction before they saw the ropefloat already descending, packed to the hilt with woodsfolk.

Now what would they do? They needed featherwings, obviously, but would there be any to spare? It had never been part of Pino's plan that *everyone* would want to leave the city at the same time.

A small hand grasped his own. Before he could even see who it was, the person jerked him backward along the bridge. As they wove through the throngs of people, he got a glimpse of a girl's blond hair and yellow dress.

"Aki?" he said.

"This way!" she said.

She led them across a series of rope bridges, all around them people shouting and screaming. Geppetto, unable to keep up, stumbled, and both Pino and Aki helped him. His cane, however, rolled off the edge and disappeared. Another bridge not far away, fortunately with no people, collapsed and crushed a dwelling below—the people escaping with their featherwings just an instant before their home exploded in a blizzard of wood and pine needles.

Through the plumes of smoke they could hear Elendrew's incomprehensible shouts.

When they arrived at another dwelling, a small one on a thinner trunk, a bald man with sad eyes swept Aki up in his arms. Behind them flames encroached upon the bridge leading to their home. There was no going back now.

"My child!" the man exclaimed. "Where have you been? We must go now!"

She wriggled out of his embrace. "I needed to help them, Father!"

They followed her inside. The whole dwelling was one tiny room with one bed, the floor blanketed with plush purple leaves. She groped under the bed.

"I'll get us the featherwings!" she said.

"We can't take one of yours!" Pino protested.

"It's okay! We have an extra. It was . . . it was Mother's." She returned with three white packs, one of which she handed to Geppetto. "One should be okay. Pino's not too heavy. I wish I had two."

Aki's father grabbed a pack and slipped the straps over his shoulders, then quickly helped Aki do the same. He started for the door with his daughter, then, seeing Geppetto struggle with his own pack, hurriedly helped him slip it over his shoulders.

"Tighten those two straps and then pull the third one when you're in open air," he said. "Good luck!"

Then he grabbed Aki and rushed out the door. A shimmering wall of fire was halfway across the bridge. They couldn't see anything beyond it but plumes of smoke.

"Good-bye, Pino!" Aki said. "Maybe I'll see you . . ."

The rest of her parting words were lost as she and her father leaped over the side. Pino heard two pops and then the zipping of their feathers twirling through the air. He wished he could have told her he was sorry.

With the two chest straps fastened, Geppetto tried to pick up Pino, but he was too weak. Pino pushed him instead out the door. The smoke billowed into the dwelling, scorching his throat. There was nothing out there—in front of them or below—but a pulsing gray cloud.

They groped until they found the rope railing.

"You climb over first!" Pino said, coughing.

"Not without you!" Geppetto said.

"I'll climb over next! Then we'll jump together!"

Reluctantly Geppetto climbed over the rail, holding fast to it as he teetered on the edge of the planks. Fire crackled through the pine needle roof. Most of the platform was ablaze, and Pino felt the heat pulsing the air like a living thing, hot on his cheeks and his neck. All around them burning wood crackled and hissed.

Pino scrambled over the rope next to Geppetto. He reached for him, stretching to grab hold of Geppetto's shirt—and then suddenly, before his grasping fingers could find purchase, the rope railing snapped and gave way.

And they both fell.

CHAPTER FOURTEEN

For a few terrible seconds Pino fell alone through a gray world—a haze of smoke and ash that burned in his lungs and seared his eyes. Through teary vision he could not see Geppetto. He could not see the ground. He could not see the dwelling where they'd stood or even the tree. He saw only shifting gray vapors, making him wonder if he'd already died.

His papa had told him about dying. He'd told him people were here and then they weren't. But he'd never told him what the people who died saw. Maybe this was it. Maybe they went to a gray place.

The moment lasted only a few heartbeats, and then he burst from the smoke and plummeted in open air.

He coughed and blinked away the tears in his eyes. Not far away, just beyond his grasp, Geppetto also fell—on his back, looking up at Pino with astonishment, his clothes fluttering. Pino could not reach him. Even worse, their descent seemed to be drifting them farther apart.

"Pino!" Geppetto cried.

They fell past white clouds of featherwings, woodsfolk in their slow drift to the ground. They fell through webs of branches, some that came dangerously close. They fell through wisps of fog. They fell faster and faster, the cool air numbing cheeks and ears, and Pino knew it was only a matter of time before they reached the ground.

Without featherwings of his own, he'd never survive. Geppetto was so far away. He had his hand on the strap that would release the featherwings, but he wasn't pulling it.

By shifting his body, leaning this way or that, Pino realized he could slightly alter the course of his fall. It was tricky, because too much leaning sent him spinning, but if he tilted just right, he angled toward Geppetto. He stretched out his arms. His papa stretched out in return. They were only inches away.

Then a thick tree branch appeared out of the mist, directly in their path.

At the last second Pino jerked backward, the branch grazing his nose. Geppetto, who hadn't reacted as quickly, wasn't nearly as lucky: The branch thumped his shoulder, sending him flying in another direction. The gap between them grew.

Out of the mist Pino finally saw the ground rising to meet them, a black mouth opening to swallow them whole.

"Pull the strap!" he cried.

"No!" Geppetto shouted back.

"Pull it!"

Geppetto shook his head and attempted to adjust his fall, bobbling, slowly drifting toward Pino. The ground was so close. Pino tucked in his arms and legs and leaned forward, slicing through the air like a blade. He was moving so fast that he knew there was a chance he'd fly right past Geppetto, but there was no time.

They fell past the last of the branches. The long trunks of the giant trees loomed around them. The ground was so close Pino could now see individual leaves and mossy green stones.

Pino realized at the last moment that he hadn't aimed well enough—he was going to fly right past Geppetto.

He twisted, stretching his arm as far as it would go, reaching out his hand.

Geppetto grasped for him. They streaked past each other. Pino saw his papa's anguished face.

Then—with a last stretch—Geppetto grabbed his finger. Not just any finger. The first finger of his right hand, the one turning into wood. Geppetto grabbed tight, and just for a moment Pino saw the startled look on Geppetto's face.

Then Geppetto pulled them together. Pino hugged both arms and both legs around his papa's body and closed his eyes, sure that it was too late, that they were going to hit the ground.

The strap was pulled.

There was a fluttering whirl as the feathers shot out of the pack, jerking them backward, gravity tugging at their feet. Pino felt his stomach drop and Geppetto's arms pressing into his back.

Then, as the featherwings did what they were intended to do, Pino and Geppetto soared through the forest.

It was either the speed of their fall or the sudden breeze that swirled from below, but their featherwings carried them much farther than Pino had expected. He'd been waiting with his eyes closed for the bone-jarring impact seconds after the featherwings opened, but when that didn't happen, he opened his eyes.

They swooped over the forest floor like an ungainly bird, dodging the massive trunks. Down here, in the thick forest, it was darker than up high. Craning his neck, Pino saw Geppetto working the braided cords that led into the whirling feathers above them, tugging one way, then the other.

Up high there had been few birds, but now many birds fluttered out of the trees at their approach. The trunks passed in a blur. They lost altitude, the ground, littered with leaves and pine needles, getting ever closer to Pino's feet.

Finally, as they were about to touch ground, Geppetto yanked back on the cords, trying to slow their speed. It was nearly perfectly done—Pino was impressed at how well his papa used the featherwings, having never used them before— but Geppetto still collapsed with a painful cry when all their weight came down on his knees.

Pino rolled off of him, spitting out a mouthful of dirt, and immediately sprang back to his papa. The featherwings floated over their heads, still tugging at the straps attached to his shoulders.

"Papa!" Pino said.

"I'm—I'm all right, boy," Geppetto said, holding one of his knees, his face screwed up in pain. "Just . . . help me undo this."

It took a bit of work, but Pino managed to get the straps of the featherwings off Geppetto's shoulders. The featherwings, buoyed by a bit of breeze, floated some distance away until they were snagged by a thorny yellow bush. Pino helped a wincing Geppetto rise to a sitting position. There was no one else around. The breeze that had carried them to this place must have carried the other featherwings somewhere else.

"Whew," Geppetto said, wiping the sweat off his forehead with his sleeve. "When we landed, it was like I was carrying a house." Then he looked at Pino with concern. "Let me see your hand, Pino."

Pino's right hand was slightly behind him, just out of

Geppetto's sight. He didn't move. "It's okay, Papa. It's—it's better now."

"Let me see it."

"It was just, um, covered with some tree sap."

"Pino—"

"We should get up, Papa. We should—"

Before Pino could react, Geppetto seized Pino's right hand and jerked it into plain sight. When he got a good look at it, he shook his head in befuddlement. But then he touched it, and his befuddlement changed first to astonishment, then dismay, then anguish.

"It's okay, Papa," Pino insisted. "It'll get better."

"When did this happen?"

"I don't know. After the cave."

"How?"

Pino felt tears springing into his eyes, and he forced them back. "I don't know, Papa. I don't know."

"Oh, boy, don't get upset. I'm just trying to understand."

"I didn't wish for it. It just happened."

"It's all right."

"I promise!" Pino insisted. "I just looked and there it was."

"Really, boy. It's all right."

"Please don't get rid of me, Papa!"

Geppetto, who'd been reaching to comfort Pino, froze. He gaped in astonishment, then slowly lifted his hand over his heart as if he'd been shot.

"Pino," he said, "my dear boy, I would *never* do such a thing. Get rid of you? Why would you say that?"

"I don't know."

"Do you think so little of me?"

"No."

"Then why do you say it? *Why?*"

Pino pulled his hand away, gazing down at his wooden finger with shame. His vision blurred with his tears, and he felt them fall hot on his cheeks. "I just thought," he began hesitatingly, "I just thought if I was turning back into wood—I thought you wouldn't want me anymore."

When he looked at Geppetto, he found that now it was his papa who had tears in his eyes. It was not the first time he remembered his papa crying, but it was the first time his papa made no effort to wipe them away and dismiss them as a bit of wood shavings in his eyes. His chin trembling, Geppetto stared for a long time, the two of them surrounded by all those giant trees, then he grabbed Pino and hugged him fiercely.

"Oh, my dear child," he said. "My child, my son, you are all that I have. I love you more than life itself. There is nothing that could change that. Nothing."

They talked about Pino's wooden finger a bit more, and since neither of them could quite pin down *why* it was happening, they decided it would probably be best if Pino didn't use his special gift unless it was absolutely necessary for their survival. Since his finger had been fine for months, Geppetto reasoned the problem must have had something to do with Pino's newfound talent. What else could it be?

The forest darkened considerably, the air growing heavy and moist. They debated whether to seek out the woodsfolk again but in the end decided they were probably better off striking out on their own. They expected a good deal of anger would be directed at Pino for enabling Elendrew to destroy their city in the trees, so there was no sense chancing a confrontation. Geppetto was quite insistent about it.

"But I helped her," Pino said. "I helped her walk. I just don't understand why she wasn't happy."

Geppetto shook his head sadly. "Some people can never be happy, Pino. They're always going to see what they don't have rather than what they do. You could have given her the gift of flight, and she would have complained about the size of her wings. And she went bad long ago, I think. Anger will do that to you. When your heart is full of rage all the time, eventually there's no room for anything else."

Pino considered this a moment. "The woodsfolk . . . do you think what they did was wrong?"

"Right, wrong, who's to say? I think they thought what they did was right. Sometimes right and wrong depends on who's saying it."

"But they loved her," Pino insisted. "They really did love her."

"Yes, I think so. But no matter how much they loved Elendrew, it wouldn't have changed anything for her. The problem was she didn't love herself." He sighed. "Anyway, I think we'd better push on. We're on the other side of the bad woods now. Maybe we can just survive on our own. We'll head west—toward the mountains."

It made Pino sad, thinking he'd never see Aki again, but he supposed he deserved it. Once again he'd tried to use his gift to help someone, and it had only turned out badly. He didn't need his papa to tell him not to use his gift. He'd decided all on his own that he'd never bring anything made of wood to life for as long as he lived—only bad things came of it.

Besides, real human boys couldn't do it, so why should he? If he wanted to be just like other boys, then he at least needed to act like them.

Within minutes Pino felt raindrops on his cheeks, and not long after that the trickle turned into a torrential downpour. They hid in the hollow of an old stump. By the time the storm had passed, it was dusk, so they bedded down there for the night. They were hungry and wet, and though the mossy ground inside the stump was soft, it also smelled bad.

If this was how it was going to be, Pino didn't think much of his papa's plan to strike out on their own.

The next morning was better. The sun pierced the trees, their path dappled with golden shadows. Birds sang merrily. They soon came to a trickling brook, where Geppetto used a makeshift net from a leafy branch to ensnare some shimmering, pink-scaled fish. The fish were tiny, not much bigger than Pino's pinkie finger, but they were also plentiful. After cooking them over a roaring fire—Geppetto showed him how to start one using dry twigs and some stones—they didn't taste bad either. If nothing else, their stomachs were full.

For the next few weeks the two of them traveled through the forest, Geppetto slowly gaining his strength, Pino learning how to fish and hunt. With some sharpened sticks they were able to kill some rabbits and even once a deer, and they spiced up these meals with roots and berries that Geppetto taught him were fine to eat. It was a wonderful time for Pino, just being with his papa.

Besides how to survive in the forest, Geppetto had many other lessons for Pino. He taught him how to add and subtract. He taught him about the planets and the stars. He taught Pino anything Pino wanted to learn, and since Pino had many questions, it seemed they were always talking. His wooden finger was getting slowly worse, spreading up to his knuckle, but it was happening so gradually that Geppetto didn't seem to notice, or if he did, he didn't mention it. What could they do but hope it went away?

All the while they drew closer to the mountains—not because they wished to live there, but because it was as good a place to head as any, and Geppetto explained it was better for a man to be heading *somewhere* rather than *nowhere*, simply because a man who was heading somewhere had a little spring in his step.

And when Geppetto was fully recovered, he certainly didn't seem to lack for a spring in his step. He laughed often and heartily. He sang old songs his own papa had taught him, teaching Pino to sing along. Sometimes instead of singing, he whistled, and when Pino tried to join him, he found all he could do was make the sound of whispering air.

"Could you teach me that, Papa?" he asked.

Geppetto looked at him with a glimmer of delight in his eyes. "What's that, boy? Ah, you mean whistling?"

Pino nodded. They were in the foothills of the mountains now, following a grassy bank of a stream up into the forest. Water trickled over rocks worn smooth. The light was fading, so they would have to make camp soon.

With winter approaching, the nights were already getting colder, so it was important to find a good camp each night, someplace where it was easy to keep a fire going. The trees in this place were still tall, but nowhere near the giants they'd passed through weeks earlier. Now Pino could actually see the sky, a sky that was laced with pinks and purples as the sunset slipped away.

"Yes, it is good to whistle," Geppetto said, stepping over a clump of grass. "Whistling is useful for many things. For song, yes, but also to call out to others."

"Like if I need help?" Pino said.

"Yes, that would be one reason. You could whistle if you needed my help. Here, let me show you. Form your mouth into an O, like this."

Try as he might, though, Pino just couldn't get it. Perhaps he might have gotten it if he'd gone on trying the rest of that night, but they'd walked only a few minutes when Geppetto stopped, grabbing Pino by the arm. He looked alarmed.

"What is—," Pino began.

Geppetto hushed him by raising a finger sharply to his lips. They stood motionless, a hint of breeze rustling the trees, then Pino heard what Geppetto heard: someone singing. It was a woman approaching the stream from the other side.

Panicked, Geppetto tugged him into the trees, where they hid behind the trunk of the thickest tree close to the bank.

A few seconds later a woman emerged from the shadows on the other side of the stream, approaching from up the hill. Their angle was such that they could see her only in profile, her left side, but Pino still got a good enough look— of curly red hair and freckled skin—that he recognized her immediately.

It was the woman he'd seen in the cave, swirling in the blue light.

He'd gotten only a glimpse of her before, but now that he saw her in person, he could see that she was exquisitely beautiful. Her long, curly hair, flowing all the way down her back, was as bright red as ripe cherries. She had high cheekbones and a pointed chin, and the freckles on her cheeks, which might have been a flaw on someone else, were perfect on her—like chocolate sprinkles on white frosting.

She carried a copper flask. Her green dress was simple, a

single piece of fabric that covered her legs all the way down to the ankles. The only odd thing about her was the strange way she tilted her head as she leaned over the bank to fill her flask.

Pino turned to tell his papa that he'd seen the woman before, but the words died in his throat when he saw the look on Geppetto's face. The way Geppetto was staring at her, with such awe and amazement, had Pino wondering if maybe Geppetto had seen her before too.

Closer, Pino could make out the words of her song. She was singing about a man she'd loved who'd been lost in a storm while sailing on the sea. Pino had heard his papa sing the same song. He'd even learned to sing it himself. Part of the song was from the woman's point of view, staring out at the waves, and the other was from the man's as he clung to the remains of his ship.

When the redheaded woman reached the part in the song where it was the man singing about the woman he'd never see again, Pino was startled when Geppetto suddenly sang along with her.

They managed only a few words together, then the woman scrambled backward, dropping the flask in the creek. It clattered against a stone and lodged itself next to a log, water rushing over it.

Geppetto stepped from behind the trunk. "Please don't be frightened, signora. You have the voice of an angel, and I mean you no . . . I mean you no . . ."

Harm. Geppetto may have whispered the final word, or Pino may simply have imagined he did, but either way the word vanished as he and Geppetto gaped at the woman on the other side of the creek. Now Pino knew why she had tilted her head just so, in that awkward way, as she filled her flask. She hadn't wanted to see her own reflection, at least not the right side.

For though half her face was perfect, the other half was terribly scarred—so many ridges and grooves and so much discoloration that the right side of her face didn't look like a face at all.

It looked like a mask.

CHAPTER FIFTEEN

Geppetto and the scarred woman stared at each other across the narrow gulf of the stream.

A sudden breeze, cooler than even moments before, raised goose bumps on the backs of Pino's arms. In the fading light shadows danced on the rippling water like black scarves. Pino could not tell if the scarring on the woman's face was from a fire or from a knife, but whatever had done it, the skin there now looked more like scales than flesh, hard and angular rather than soft and rounded.

"Who—who are you?" the woman asked.

Geppetto swallowed. "I'm sorry to have frightened you."

"What do you want?"

"Nothing, signora," Geppetto said. "We mean you no harm. We are merely poor travelers, my son and I. My name is . . . Teppo. And my son—come out, boy, it's all right—his name is Francisco."

Not understanding why his papa had lied, Pino stepped next to Geppetto. He was careful to keep his right hand behind him at all times so she wouldn't see his wooden finger.

It must have occurred to the woman that the scarred half of her face was visible to them, because she turned her head. Thinking back to the cave, Pino realized he'd seen her only from the left side, but he also remembered how pure her smile had been when she'd looked at Geppetto.

While she spoke, she leaned over the stream and fished out her flask. "If you're looking for a place to stay for the night," she said, "the town of Deltora is just north of here. You can cross just up ahead. If you walk east a little ways, you'll come to a road—there's an inn there you can stay in for the night. They'd— they'd be glad to have you. If you can pay." She added the last part with a bit of a warning.

"Is that where you live?" Geppetto asked.

Pino realized that if the woman had been smiling at Geppetto in that vision in the cave, then he must have been smiling back. He could hear that smile in his voice now. If the woman's scars bothered him, he certainly wasn't showing it.

She looked at him with suspicion. "No," she said. "I live in Deltora, but not at the inn."

"Ah," Geppetto said.

They stared at each other in silence, then the woman broke away her gaze awkwardly, quickly filling her flask. As she stood, the water sloshed onto the bank.

"I really must be going," she said.

"Please," Geppetto said, though Pino wasn't sure what he was saying "please" for.

"Good luck," she said.

She darted into the forest, no longer moving with the stately grace she'd displayed before, but with the kind of slinking defeat of a wounded animal. Pino realized he couldn't let her go. He liked how his papa sounded when he spoke to her. He wanted to hear that sound in his voice again.

"Could we stay with you?" Pino called after her. "We don't have any money. We're very poor."

"Son!" Geppetto admonished. "Your manners need much—"

"We won't be any trouble!" Pino added.

"Boy, that's quite enough!" Geppetto snapped.

"No, it's all right," the woman said, turning back to them. She regarded them for a long time with one eye, the scarred part of her face shrouded by the shadows of the trees. "If money is a hardship for you, my home is open to you both. Winter's coming on, and it gets quite cold here at night. I could not stand the thought of you out in it without a roof over your heads."

"I—I wouldn't want you to go to any trouble on our behalf," Geppetto said.

"Oh?" she said. "Is it really that much trouble to open my door to those in need?"

"N-n-no," Geppetto stammered, "that's not what I—"

"I may be ugly, but that does not mean I am cruel."

Geppetto, looking pained, placed his hand over his heart in the same way he had covered his heart when Pino had mistakenly thought Geppetto would want to get rid of him.

"Signora," he said slowly, "I would *never* call you ugly. You have an uncommon beauty."

She snorted derisively, but Geppetto merely went on looking at her, staring so long and steadfastly that she finally looked away. It was difficult to tell in the twilight, but Pino thought she might be blushing.

"Well then," she said stiffly. "If you're going to come, you better get on with it. Like I said, there's a way to cross upstream. I'm—I'm going to have some vegetable stew tonight. It's not much, but you're welcome to join me."

"We would be most grateful," Geppetto said.

* * *

Her name, they soon learned, was Olivia. She lived in a cottage at the edge of the woods, not far from the inn of which she had spoken—an inn whose bawdy guests could be heard singing loud and off-key long into the night. The town of Deltora, inhabited mostly by goat herders and fur trappers, could be seen in the lighted windows sprinkling the hillside at the base of the mountains. They were close enough to the mountains now that Pino could see the star-studded sky yawning above the dark peaks.

When they asked her how many people lived there, she told them she didn't really know. Not more than a hundred, surely. Though she'd been born in Deltora, she'd only recently returned, and she seldom went into town. She had a cow for milk, a few chickens for eggs, and a bountiful vegetable garden that was her pride and joy. What more could a person want?

Neither Geppetto nor Pino asked her how she'd gotten her scars. Pino noticed that she always made sure to stand on their right. He didn't mind so much, except he always had to make sure Papa was between them so she wouldn't notice his right hand.

The stew, a wonderful mixture of vegetables with garlic and other spices, was the best meal they'd had in a month, but the long pauses in the conversation made it difficult to relax. After dinner, sitting by the fire crackling in the hearth, they began to talk more freely.

She even flashed a few smiles, mostly at something funny Geppetto said, and it warmed Pino's heart. Even better was the way Geppetto smiled back. It wasn't the same way he smiled at Pino. It was . . . different.

Getting used to going by Francisco was certainly hard, but he figured his papa had a good reason for it. His papa always did. Nor were their names his only lies. He did tell her they'd been forced to leave home because they'd lost everything in a fire, but he didn't tell her *what* had caused the fire. He told her nothing of wooden puppets coming to life or angry villagers or anything at all of their adventures in the treetops.

Pino wished he could just tell Olivia the truth. Besides, keeping his right hand out of sight all the time was exhausting. He could barely think of anything else. Fortunately, Olivia rescued him by saying it was getting late and they'd best all retire for the night.

"I wish you'd sing for us first," Geppetto said.

"Oh, no," Olivia said.

"Just one song," Geppetto pleaded. "Your voice—it is so lovely. It would be nice to be carried into pleasant dreams by it."

"That's very kind of you, but no. No, I don't sing for anyone. Not on purpose, anyway. Not anymore."

"Anymore?" Geppetto said.

She frowned. "Yes. That is why I left Deltora so many years ago. I left to sing. And I did. I was quite famous, actually."

"Then why—"

"Let me show you where you'll sleep," she said abruptly. "I'm sure you're tired."

The cottage sported only one bedroom, but there was a loft reachable by ladder, and she gave them heavy blankets to ward off the cold. If he'd come straight from his old bed, Pino would have been disappointed, but after sleeping in dank caves and moldy stumps the past few weeks, a dry loft and a few good blankets were wonderful.

It rained hard during the night, a constant drumming on the thatched roof, but not a drop reached them inside. Pino, worried about his hand, lay awake next to his snoring papa for a long time, running his thumb along the wooden fingers—two of them now, the first and the second. The ridge where the flesh turned to wood was sensitive to the touch; if he pressed too hard in that place, it stung. The wood was definitely spreading.

In the morning Pino woke to the smell of freshly baked bread. It was no longer raining, and golden spears of light brightened the loft. He heard the clanging of a pail outside and then Olivia murmuring. When Pino rolled over, he saw that Geppetto was sewing a piece of cloth with a needle he'd made from a twig and some coarse thread he must have gotten from unraveling part of his own shirt.

"Papa?" Pino said.

Geppetto smiled at him. "I made something for you while you were sleeping," he said, handing him what appeared to be a white glove. "Probably best to keep it out of sight for now, eh?"

It was a crude thing, obviously made from part of the tail of Geppetto's shirt, but it fit Pino's hand snugly. More importantly, it completely hid his wooden fingers.

"Thank you," Pino said.

"I'm sure your hand will be better soon, boy," Geppetto said, though he didn't sound all that sure. "This is just to be safe."

"Safe?"

"That's right. I'm sure you noticed how I didn't tell Olivia the truth. We don't want anyone to know about us. About you. About what you can do. It would just make people ask questions."

Pino nodded. "Papa?"

"Yes, boy?"

"Do you like Olivia?"

Geppetto turned bashful, smiling a secret smile. "Yes, I think I do. I think I like her quite a bit."

"So we're staying here, then?"

"I hope so, boy. I really do."

When they climbed down the ladder, they found Olivia entering the cottage with a pail of milk. The brisk morning air shook off the last remnants of Pino's sleepiness. Olivia smiled at them—or rather, smiled mostly at Geppetto—in much the same way Geppetto had smiled when Pino asked him if he liked Olivia. Pino also noticed that she'd done her best to comb her hair over the right side of her face.

"I baked you some rolls," she said.

"They smell wonderful," Geppetto said. "Sorry I didn't come down to lend a hand. I don't think I've ever slept so soundly."

"It's no bother," she said. "You must be exhausted from all your travels. I have milk and eggs, too. Come, sit."

If the previous night's supper was the best they'd had in a month, the breakfast was even better, especially the moist, warm bread that dissolved like sugar in their mouths. Pino watched as Geppetto and Olivia stole quick glances at each other. When they'd eaten their fill, Geppetto went out to chop firewood—insisting, over her objections, he had to earn their breakfast—and left Pino alone with her.

She refilled his cup of milk. "You are lucky to have such a wonderful man as your papa, Francisco," she said. "You know, there's a good school in town. If you—if you decide to stay for a while, that is."

"I think we're going to stay," Pino said, though he wasn't sure about school. He'd never been to a school and didn't know why he'd want to go when he could learn everything he needed from his papa. "I like it here."

"I'm very glad," she said.

Pino reached for his cup and was so distracted by talking to her, trying to be nice so she wouldn't have a reason to want them to leave, that he reached with his right hand instead of his left. Even wearing the glove, he'd tried to use just his left, since it seemed funny to be wearing a glove at the table. And of course she noticed.

"That's an interesting glove," she said.

He took an extra-long drink of milk, then wiped off his chin. "Thank you. Papa—Papa made it for me."

"I don't remember you wearing it yesterday."

"I wasn't. I didn't. I—I only wear it sometimes. My hand, it got burned."

Olivia looked concerned. "Oh no. You should let me see it. I might be able—"

"No, no, it's all right. It's okay. It's getting better."

"Are you sure? It wouldn't hurt to show it to me. Here, let me see it."

She reached for his hand, and Pino jerked it under the table. "It's okay," he said.

"Francisco—"

"I better go help Papa," he said, heading for the door. "He—he still gets tired quickly."

Before she could answer, he headed for the door. He hoped that would be the last time she asked about his hand.

He hoped for it, but something told him it wouldn't be.

CHAPTER SIXTEEN

The next few weeks were some of the best of Pino's life. It had been good traveling with his papa, joking and laughing about the stupidest things, as only a father and son can, but there was something about adding Olivia to the mix that was even better.

She didn't laugh at all of Geppetto's jokes—in fact, most of the time she just wrinkled her nose as if to say what a silly man he was—and sometimes she scolded Pino when he didn't eat all his food or if he tracked mud into the cottage, but it was still much better having her around.

It was like they were a family. A real family, just like Pino had always wanted, with a father *and* a mother.

They settled into a routine, with Geppetto and Pino pitching in with the chores. Geppetto even started carving again, using tools borrowed from the inn. When he'd made some chairs and a couple of rocking horses, he ventured into town to sell them. Pino carved some things too, mostly toy animals, but he didn't go into town. Neither did Olivia, though when Geppetto started earning some money, she gave him a list of things to buy—mostly fruit, flour, and various spices. Geppetto bought her flowers almost every day.

It was during one of his trips into town that Olivia finally got a glimpse of what was happening to Pino's hand. It wasn't because he wasn't wearing the glove. It was because the wood had spread *beyond* the glove without his realizing it, nearly up to his wrist, and she saw it when he was reaching to grab the milk pail from underneath the cow and the cloth slipped slightly.

"Oh my word," she said. "Your—your skin."

"It's all right," Pino said. He hurried toward the cottage, the milk sloshing in the pail. The cow, uninterested, went on munching the grass. It was sunset, the sky a swirling mix of oranges and reds, but even late in the day frost still glazed the ground. It was getting colder.

She followed on his heels. "What's wrong with it?"

"I told you. It got burned."

"That was a strange-looking burn."

"It's getting better. It really is."

"Hmm. I have a cream that could help with the healing. Perhaps if you let me—"

"No," Pino insisted.

They were in the cottage now. He set the pail on the table, then pulled up his glove as far as it would go, which was just barely far enough to cover the hardened ridge between the flesh and the wood. She closed the door behind them and regarded him quietly for a while, arms crossed, lips pursed. Then she turned to the window. The setting sun, a yellow orb filling the paned glass, gave her a golden silhouette.

"Don't you like me, Francisco?" she asked.

"I like you."

"Don't you want us all to be happy?"

"Yes."

"Well, we can't be happy unless we tell each other things. We can't be happy if we're always keeping secrets from each other."

"But you're keeping a secret," Pino insisted. "You—you don't tell us how . . . how . . ." He started boldly, but when it came time to say the words "how you got those scars," he couldn't bring himself to do it.

It didn't matter. When she looked at him again, she pointed at the right side of her face, that patchwork of skin painted with crimson light from the setting sun. "This, you mean?" she said. "All right, I'll tell you. I'll tell your papa, too, when he comes back. A man did this to me."

"A man?" Pino said.

"I told you I was a singer. He was . . . someone who helped me. Who was my teacher. He also arranged all of my concerts. We were very happy for a while, but . . . but he drank, you see. And when he drank, he sometimes got angry. One time he got very angry, and he did this to me."

"I'm sorry," Pino said.

Olivia shrugged. "He went to prison and I returned home. I—I couldn't get up there in front of people anymore. I couldn't stand the way they looked at me. I thought it would be better here, but . . . well, it doesn't matter. Now that you're here, I don't need to go into town at all. Teppo can do that." She stepped close to him and, before he could pull away, took hold of his gloved hand. "Please let me see it, Francisco. Please trust me."

He was scared of what she was going to do, but when she tugged at the glove, he didn't stop her. As the flesh that was now wood came into view, he watched her eyes, watched how they widened. The change had come to his entire hand now. She touched it, yanking her hand back as if scalded.

"It's wood!" she exclaimed.

"Yes," Pino said.

"Does it hurt?"

"No."

"Does it . . . feel different?"

Pino shrugged. "It feels like wood."

"Was it always like that?"

"No. Well, yes. In the beginning. But then it wasn't. Now it's going back."

She looked confused, so with a sigh he went ahead and told her his story. He started at the beginning, though he didn't tell her all the adventures he'd had before he became a real boy. He simply told her that he'd been a puppet in the beginning, and then he became flesh and blood. He told her about his special gift, about how he'd brought a dead tree to life and made a wooden suit for Elendrew. He told her how that was when the hand had started to change, so he and Geppetto decided that it must have something to do with his gift.

By the time he'd told her the whole story, the sky outside the window had darkened. Geppetto would be home soon. Pino had felt anxious when he started, not sure how she'd react, but by the end he was very glad he'd told her. And if they were a family now, then what was wrong with telling her? Maybe his papa would tell her their real names, too. She was right. They shouldn't keep secrets.

At some point they'd moved to the table. Olivia hadn't bothered to light a candle, so the room was dark, her face veiled with shadows.

"So you can make things out of wood and bring them to life?" she asked.

"Yes," he said.

"This puppet of Antoinette," she said. "Did she look much like the real thing?"

"I don't know. Papa thought so."

"So people thought she was real?"

"Well . . ."

"I bet you could do an even better job this time."

Pino didn't understand. "But I don't want to make another Antoinette. I don't want to use my gift at all."

"I bet you could even make one of me," Olivia continued as if she hadn't heard.

"You?"

She rose from the table and went to the window, hardly more than a dark shape in front of the glass. "Yes," she said softly. "Yes, you could make one of me. One with—with a whole face. One just as beautiful as I once was."

"But I can't—I can't make it speak —"

"It doesn't matter. It doesn't have to have a voice. Don't you see? *I* have a voice. She could go into town, and people would see her and know that I was beautiful again." Her voice had taken on a dreamy quality, as if she'd forgotten where she was. "Maybe I could even sing again. She would stand on the stage while I hid behind the curtains and sang. Then I could be as I once was."

"But it wouldn't be you. It would be a puppet."

"It doesn't matter. Other people would *think* it was me."

Pino regretted he'd ever said anything to her. "No," he said. "I won't do it."

She turned and looked at him, her eyes invisible in the darkness. "Don't you want me to be happy, Francisco?"

"Yes. But—"

"Don't you want your papa to be happy?"

Pino hesitated. He didn't understand what she was trying to do. "I want him to be happy. He's the one who told me—"

"I'm sure he told you not to use your gift," she said. "And after this last time you won't have to use it again, I promise. He doesn't have to know. You'll work on it when he goes into town. We'll surprise him at the end, and I'm sure he'll be happy for me."

"I don't think—"

"YOU WILL DO IT!" she bellowed.

In all the weeks they'd lived with her, Olivia had never once raised her voice. She'd spoken sternly. She'd scolded him. But shouted? No, she'd never once shouted, and it wasn't just a shout; it was a full-throated roar. It shocked him, and it must have shocked her, too, because for a long time she simply stood there in the near darkness, filling the silence with the sound of her own harried breathing. Finally her breathing slowed and she spoke more softly.

"You will do it," she warned, "or I will stop loving your papa."

CHAPTER SEVENTEEN

The next morning it snowed. It was just a light dusting that powdered the grass and the trees, but it was a harbinger of things to come. It snowed each day for the rest of the week, and each time the snow came down heavier. Soon the landscape was draped in white. Winter was no longer knocking on the door. It had arrived.

Seeing no other choice, Pino spent every moment that Geppetto was out of the cottage working on a puppet for Olivia. There were lots of opportunities because Olivia thought up many excuses to send Geppetto to town—for sugar or flour or something of the like—and of course he went into town plenty of his own accord too, saying he wanted to try to sell as many of his carvings as he could before it got so cold that venturing out was unbearable.

Pino worked in Olivia's room, on her soft, downy bed, which made it easier to hide the puppet when Olivia spotted Geppetto's bundled form clomping up the road. The bedroom was the one room where Geppetto didn't go. If the door was shut, he'd never see what was inside.

The puppet itself came along nicely. There was lots of wood about, and whenever Geppetto was gone, Pino had his choice of the tools. These tools weren't borrowed, but owned, since

Geppetto had used some of his first earnings to buy them. It was much easier to make the puppet look like a person when you had that person sitting in front of you. When he'd finished the face, Olivia wept tears of joy.

He started to think that maybe it wasn't such a bad idea making the puppet for Olivia. In a way, she was just like him. She wanted to feel more like a normal person. What could be wrong with that?

The only real problem were Pino's hands. Since both of them had turned into wood, it was much harder to hold the chisels and the rasps.

Now and then Pino caught Geppetto and Olivia kissing, a chaste sort of kiss that quickly ceased when they noticed Pino. Whenever he doubted whether he was doing the right thing with the puppet, Pino thought about those kisses. About how happy his papa looked.

After the puppet's face was done, the rest of the body came much faster. The closer he got to the finish, the more nervous Pino became. What would his papa do when he found it? He dreaded having to face him.

It turned out the moment came sooner than they'd anticipated. Pino was only a day or two from finishing the puppet when the front door suddenly swung open—a mere ten minutes after Geppetto had set out for town.

"I forgot the new chair," Geppetto said, dusting the snow off his wool coat. "Silly me. I can't very well sell it if I . . ." He trailed off when he saw, through the open door into Olivia's room, what was on her bed.

"Teppo!" Olivia cried, leaping to her feet.

She'd been sitting in a chair next to the bed, with Pino sitting in a chair on the other side. The puppet of Olivia, already dressed in one of her finest blue dresses, lay on the bed between them.

"What's—what's going on here?" Geppetto said.

She bustled over to him, taking him by the arms, trying to ward him away from her room. "What? Nothing!"

Geppetto pushed her gently aside. "What's that on your bed?"

"That? It's—it's supposed to be a surprise."

"Oh no . . ."

"Teppo . . ."

But he wasn't listening. He'd already stepped past her into the bedroom, gazing upon the puppet with the same horror with which he'd looked upon the puppet of Antoinette months earlier. Pino knew, right away, he'd made a terrible mistake. He wished he could take it all back. Outside the snow fell heavier than ever on Olivia's pasture.

"I'm sorry, Papa," Pino said.

Geppetto shook his head. "Why?"

"He did it for me," Olivia explained. "He did it because I asked him. It's—it's almost finished, Teppo. It's almost finished, and then he can bring it to life."

"But for what reason?" Geppetto asked. "A puppet of *you*? It makes no sense."

"It's not me," Olivia said. "It's a *better* me. It's me as I *should* be—still beautiful, still a woman who can turn people's heads."

Geppetto looked sad. "You *are* beautiful, Olivia."

"Don't be foolish," she scoffed.

"I'm not. It's what I think."

"Then you're an idiot." She pointed at the scarred half of her face. "Don't you see this? Are you *blind*?"

"But the puppet won't change—"

"Of course it won't change my scars! That doesn't matter! It will change what people *think* about me! *That's all that matters!*"

She was screaming, fists clenched and pink color spreading up her neck into her face. Strangely, the scarred half of her face didn't become pink, but darker, nearly black. In the little bedroom, hardly big enough for the three of them, her shouts were deafening.

"Olivia," Geppetto said softly, "please be calm."

"I don't need to be calm. This is my life!"

"Olivia—"

"Francisco," Olivia said, "bring the puppet to life. It's ready."

"No," Geppetto said. "Don't do it, son. Nothing good will come of it."

"Bring it to life!" she cried.

"Has he told you about his hands? What using his gift does to him?"

"It's only *once!* Just do it, Francisco!"

Pino was afraid to move. They'd been a family, the three of them, and now it was all unraveling. Olivia pushed past Geppetto and fell to her knees, grasping Pino's shoulder, fingernails digging into his skin.

"Please!" she begged. "Please bring it to life."

"Stop!" Geppetto said.

"If you do this for me, I'll love you!" she continued. "I'll love you both! I'll be the mother you always wanted!"

Geppetto shouted at her again to stop, but she didn't listen. She went on pleading with Pino until her words ran together, not making any sense, until Geppetto grabbed her and pried her away. She kicked and screamed and flailed at him. One of her fingernails slashed his neck, drawing blood, and Geppetto tossed her onto the bed.

She landed right on top of the puppet, their noses inches apart. She gazed at it a long time, then started weeping.

"Look at me," she said. "So beautiful . . . so very beautiful . . ."

"Olivia," Geppetto whispered. "Olivia . . . please . . ."

He reached for her, touching her gently on the shoulder, and she slapped his hand away.

"Get out!" she screamed. "Get out, the both of you!"

Geppetto looked stricken. "Olivia!"

"Get out! Get out now!"

"It's the middle of a snowstorm!"

"I don't care! You're not welcome here! I hate you! I hate you both!"

In a soothing voice Geppetto tried to reason with her, but it only made Olivia more enraged. She came at him in a howling fury, clawing and scratching at his face, and it was all Geppetto could do to keep her at bay. Then she began grabbing whatever she could find and hurling it at them—a vase, several plates, even a lantern. A cup smashed through the window, shattering the glass, and chill winter air flowed into the cottage.

Nothing would dissuade her. "Out, out, out!" she cried again and again, until her beautiful voice grew hoarse. She hurled one of Geppetto's tools—a rasp he'd purchased in town only the previous week—and it struck Pino a glancing blow on the shoulder. It didn't draw any blood, but it seemed to change Geppetto.

He took Pino's hand and hurried to the loft, where he grabbed the two leather bags he'd been using to cart his wood carvings into town, shoving clothes, tools, and other items into them. Below, Olivia was cursing and weeping, but she was no longer throwing things.

When Geppetto had stuffed the bags to the brim, he had Pino put on several layers of clothes and the wool coat that matched the one Geppetto wore. Then they climbed back downstairs.

The main room was oddly quiet. The chill air whistled through what remained of the window. Snowflakes, oblivious to the tension in the cottage, floated peacefully to the earth. Stepping into the middle of the room, they saw Olivia in her bedroom, bent over the puppet. She didn't make a sound.

"Olivia?" Geppetto said.

"Out," she moaned.

"Are you sure?"

"OUT!"

Geppetto took Pino's hand and led him to the door. Olivia let loose with a terrible, mournful wail. As they stepped outside, into a white world both great in its beauty and terrible in its cold, Pino glanced over his shoulder.

Before the door shut, he got one last look at Olivia. He saw her leaning over the puppet, cupping her hands on either side of its face, her own tears falling on its wooden cheeks. She was murmuring something to it, the type of thing you would murmur to a sick child, too softly for him to make out the words.

Then a sudden gust of icy wind slammed the door.

CHAPTER EIGHTEEN

They staggered like wounded soldiers, Pino and Geppetto, over a blinding desert. It was a desert of snow instead of sand, of blistering cold instead of blistering heat, but it was a desert just the same. It soon stopped snowing, and the sun glared on the glistening white dunes, so bright Pino had to squint. The snow, though soft and billowing under their boots, smothered the life out of the world. It smothered the hills and the trees and the few cottages glimpsed amidst all that white. It even smothered their clothes, until Geppetto and Pino were part of the winter landscape too—not soldiers, but ghosts, marching in silence, alone with their own dark thoughts.

The only parts of Pino's body that weren't soon numb from the cold were his wooden hands—and he would have laughed at that if there were any laughter in him to be found. There had never been a time in his short life when he felt more desperate and afraid than he felt in that moment. He hated who he was and what he could do. If he were a normal boy, one who couldn't bring wood to life, then they would still be back at the cottage with Olivia. And Geppetto would be happy.

If he was going to turn into wood, he wished he would get it over with already. Maybe he was meant to be a puppet.

Someone else would pull his strings and make him dance, and he'd never be able to screw up anything on his own again.

For the next few weeks they did not speak about Olivia. They did not speak about much of anything. They continued west.

Fortunately, they had a little bit of money, coins Geppetto had earned from wood carving, so they did not have to sleep in the cold. They stopped occasionally in villages high in the mountains, remote places unlikely to have heard of them. Pino wore two pairs of gloves, always with long-sleeved shirts, and was careful never to give someone even a glimpse of the wood underneath. They operated under assumed names, trying each time to begin life anew, but then they'd catch an odd glance or someone would ask an unusual question, and by the crack of dawn they'd be on the road again.

It continued to snow. It snowed most of all up in the mountains, great drifts of snow that made passage nearly impossible. But they marched on regardless. They marched as if somewhere ahead, somewhere around the next bend or the next tree, they would find something to believe in again.

Finally they crested the mountains, and as they descended toward the great gray expanse of the ocean on the other side, the snow shriveled and disappeared. The air changed from freezing to chilly and damp, still cold, but at least Pino's toes weren't numb all the time.

They came to a large village on the western seashore, with big ships sailing regularly in and out of port and enough people milling the muddy streets that two more newcomers could go largely unnoticed. There was no snow at all. The moist ocean winds, Geppetto explained, made for mild winters.

They were even more in luck, because the town's wood-carver had recently passed away, and there was plenty of work to be had. Within days they had taken over the wood-carver's shop—the landlord was desperate for a new tenant and allowed them to take up residence of the slanting brick building with a small payment—and even had a few standing orders.

The town was a gritty place, populated by people who seemed cruel and joyless, but Geppetto insisted it was perfect for their needs.

"If we play it smart," said Geppetto, who now went by the name Florin, "I think we can stay here for a while. At least until we earn enough money."

Pino was about to take another bite of the chicken stew they'd made for dinner that night, when he paused, studying his papa over the top of the flickering candle. Next to them, the ocean wind whistled against the window. "Until we earn enough money for what, Papa?"

"To leave, son. To leave for another country."

"We're not staying here?"

"No. Someday someone will find out. They always do."

"Where will we go?"

Geppetto gazed out the paned window. The sky was velvet black, and the ocean was visible only as a slightly less dark expanse that stretched beneath it. "I don't know," he said. "But we'll get on one of these ships and cross the ocean to a place where no one would believe our story even if they heard it."

It was a good plan, and for several months it seemed like it would work just as Geppetto had said it would. They quietly settled into their new life, saving every spare coin for their eventual trip across the ocean, keeping to themselves except for their brief encounters with the customers. Pino always made sure to wear long-sleeved shirts and gloves. No one asked about their past. No one, as far as they could tell, suspected anything was unusual about them.

Until the dreadful day when Pino was at the market down by the docks picking up salmon for dinner.

People crowded the boardwalk, and it was so noisy that he didn't know anything was happening until he heard a woman scream.

The smell of fish was heavy on the afternoon breeze, and the sun had already sunk beneath the ocean. Pino stopped haggling with the shopkeeper and turned toward the sound. He saw the object of her terror right away, for the people were parting and spreading away from it like water rippling away from a hulking ship.

It was a black and charred thing, stumbling on footless peg legs, flapping a single arm as dark and thin as a poker. What remained of its head was a dusty gray mass, crumbling in on itself, like one of the rotten apples Pino used to see in the apple orchard not far from their old home. It was the few strands of black horsehair still attached to its scalp that made Pino finally realize what it was, and then every muscle in his body seized tight.

"Antoinette," he whispered.

For a few long, agonizing seconds he could do nothing but watch the monster he'd created—what he'd created out of love and affection for his papa—lumber along the boardwalk. It did not see him at first, and may not have if Pino had been quicker to move, but then it did, its one remaining eye fixing on him.

It stopped, stared, and then doubled its speed, heading straight for the boy.

Then Pino was running. He did not *decide* to run; one moment he was looking at the monster, and the next moment he was looking at the astonished faces of the people he passed. He ran as fast as his feet would carry him, not daring to look over his shoulder even once, running over the broken cobblestone streets all the way to the workshop and collapsing at his papa's feet.

The room stank of the lacquer his papa used to stain the furniture, and Papa, pausing mid-brushstroke on a rocking chair, reacted with surprise. A streak of brown marred his cheek.

"Pino?" he said. "What is it?"

"Papa—Papa . . . ," Pino began, but his trembling jaw wouldn't form the words.

It was no matter. Within seconds there was commotion outside, some shouts, some children crying. Papa, brush still in hand, went to the window.

"Oh no," he said.

He stepped away, his face pale. Neither of them moved. There was a dull pounding on the door and they both jumped. The doorknob rattled and jiggled but did not turn. Pino wondered why, why the thing did not open the door, until he realized that no, of course it couldn't.

It had no hands.

Geppetto gritted his teeth and grabbed his ax from the corner. He stopped at the door, hand on the rattling knob, eyes closed for quite some time. Then he tossed open the door and lunged outside. The door blocked Pino's view, but he heard it all: the sounds of struggle, a few grunts from Papa, and then the awful crunch of the ax splintering wood. The crunching came again and again, and Pino sank to the floor, pressing his face to his knees. It was the worst sound in the world, the crunching of that ax, and it went on forever.

Finally there was only Geppetto's labored breathing.

"Go home!" he shouted at the onlookers. "Go home, there's nothing of any interest here anymore!"

There were some murmurs of discontent, some shuffling feet, and then Geppetto was back in the room, slamming the door behind him. Pino looked up and saw not his papa, but a madman, wild eyed and flush faced. He looked at Pino without seeing him, then dropped the ax and lumbered to the woodstove. The morning's fire had been reduced to a scattering of orange glowing embers.

"Papa?" Pino said.

With his back to him, Pino could not make out his papa's face. Geppetto took a piece of folded yellow parchment from his front pocket, unfolded it, and studied it for a few seconds, then opened the stove door and tossed the paper inside.

"Papa," he said, "what is it?"

The paper caught fire immediately, a burst of light that set Geppetto's shadow dancing on the brick wall. The flaming paper crumpled and twisted, and when it did, Pino caught sight of a woman's eye.

CHAPTER NINETEEN

Geppetto and Pino packed in a hurry, stuffing as many of their belongings as they could into the two large bags Pino had hoped they'd never have to use again. After all, people who went on ships could take suitcases, crates even; it was only people on the run who had to pack light. He protested. He asked if they had enough money, and Geppetto said it would have to be enough. He asked why they couldn't wait until morning, but Geppetto said it would be too dangerous to wait.

News might travel slowly across great distances, he said, but in a crowded town a rumor would touch every household faster than a sudden rain.

With the evening light fading to black, Geppetto smothered the remaining embers in the stove with ash. They hadn't bothered to light a lantern, and with the fire out, most of the light came from the open door—a purple, dusky light that fell across the floor like a rug. The first sign that they had a visitor was when the light dimmed and a shadow appeared on the wood shavings coating the floor.

"Going somewhere, wood-carver?" a voice said.

It was a man standing in the doorway, visible only as a short and stout silhouette. Geppetto, cloaked in shadow, slipped the bags off his shoulders and eased them behind him.

"Oh, no," he said, "just doing a bit of tidying up before supper."

"Ah," the man said. "How fortunate for me. I'd hate to think you were leaving town just when I needed your services most."

Two more silhouettes appeared on either side of the short man, silhouettes belonging to much bigger and broader men. Geppetto fumbled to an oil lantern and lit it.

The short man was bald except for a ring of silver hair and a long black handlebar mustache that stretched straight out like the wings of a crow in flight. A gold chain dangled from one of the pockets of his suit, a suit that strained to hold in his rotund body. The two larger men, dressed in the plain gray uniform of the local police, carried rifles with bayonets.

"Do you know who I am?" the small man asked.

"Yes," Geppetto said, and Pino could hear the heaviness in his voice, "you are the town's mayor, I believe."

"That is correct." The short man smiled, and it was a tight-lipped smile that was entirely in the lips and not in the eyes at all. "I am Mayor Serro. One of my chief responsibilities is to keep the peace in our quaint little town."

"How can I help you, Signore Serro?" Geppetto asked.

"Ah, well, you see, I heard about the disturbance this afternoon," Serro said. He entered the room, the two larger men remaining in the doorway. "A very strange tale it was."

"Yes, I'm sorry for the trouble," Geppetto said. "It won't happen again."

"Oh, well, I hope it does."

Geppetto hesitated. "I'm sorry?"

Serro wiped his finger across one of the worktables, sniffed the dust that stuck to his finger, then blew it away. "It seems you have been misleading us . . . Signore Geppetto."

No one spoke for a long time. It did not shock Pino that Serro knew his papa's real name, because Serro seemed like the sort of man who would know things.

"What do you want?" Geppetto asked. "Do you want us to leave town? Because we are more than happy—"

"Oh, no, no," Serro said, "I would never ask such a fine craftsman as yourself to leave. You are probably the best thing that ever happened to our town. No, you see, I come because of a personal matter. I would like to hire you."

Pino watched as what remained of the pleasant mask Geppetto was wearing drained away. "To do what?"

Instead of answering the question, Serro looked at Pino. He stepped closer to him, running a hand through Pino's hair. The hand felt as heavy and cold as a lump of deer meat brought in from the ice box. Pino hated being touched by him, and when Serro finally dropped his hand, Pino took two steps backward. Even though both of Pino's hands were gloved, and his sleeves were tucked into them, he kept them behind his back.

"Such amazing handiwork," Serro said. "You know, my own daughter would be about his age now. Unfortunately, when she was only two, she fell from our buggy and broke her neck."

"I'm quite sorry to hear that. I'm still not sure what you think I can—"

"Oh, I think you know."

Geppetto shook his head. "It is not something I can do."

"No?" Serro gestured at Pino. "And yet, here before me is proof otherwise."

"It was merely a fluke. Made from enchanted wood I've never been able to find again."

The mayor smiled. "Once, I'd believe. But twice? We heard

what walked into the village today. That's no fluke. No, you will do this thing for me. I will pay you handsomely, of course." He signaled to one of the men at the door, who ducked briefly out of sight and reappeared with a small painting.

The man stepped into the room and held the painting for all to see. It pictured a small girl with bright red hair dressed in a green cotton dress and a matching bonnet.

"And if I refuse?" Geppetto asked.

Serro's gaze drifted to Pino. "You have a beautiful boy, signore. You know, I speak from experience when I say that it really is the worst kind of tragedy when something awful happens to your child."

Geppetto gaped. "You threaten my *son*? You, who would ask me to bring your daughter back from the dead?"

"I have said nothing of the sort," the man said. "I am only telling you what my own experience has taught me. But let me be clear, Signore Geppetto: I made my wife a promise. I promised I would keep our daughter safe. I failed. She has now succumbed to madness, passing her days in the dismal darkness of our wine cellar. Here is my chance to make it right. If you only do as I say, no harm will come to anyone."

Pino saw that a muscle in Geppetto's neck was pulsing. His jaw looked as if it had been frozen in ice. "All right," he sighed. "I seem to have no choice. It will take some time, though. If you return in a week—"

"Oh, no," Serro said, "I suspect you'd find a way to escape, even if I left my men to watch over you. No, you'll be coming with me. The jail is currently unoccupied, and there's plenty of room to work in there."

"In prison! You would treat me like a common criminal?"

Serro made a *tsk-tsk* sound. "Come now, it won't be that

bad. Unlike the poor wretches who have been there lately, you, at least, will be well fed. And I hope I don't have to remind you that you were seen killing that poor, unfortunate woman earlier today. You will have to be tried for such a crime."

"It wasn't a woman!" Geppetto cried. "It was nothing but—but—but—*wooden bones!*"

"Well, that will be for the law to decide. Of course, I am a friend of the judge, and I think I can get him to waive the charge . . . so long as you do the work I ask, of course."

Geppetto, red faced, sputtered, "But—but I need my tools!"

"My men will bring whatever you need. Pack your things."

"But we can't just leave the shop unattended! We have customers . . . work that needs to be done. . . ."

"It will be waiting for you when you return."

"Do you have no heart at all, signore?"

Finally Pino saw an ever so slight softening in Serro's eyes, and when the man spoke, his voice was tinged with the same sadness that often touched his papa's voice when he was having his worst days. "I want you to know that I am not a cruel man," Serro said. "Circumstances have forced me to be this way. I will tell you what I will do. I will leave your son to tend to your business in your absence—I'm sure, learning from you, he's become quite the wood-carver himself."

"Thank you," Geppetto said.

"But," Serro warned, leveling his plump finger at Pino, "you will be there in a week when he finishes his work, boy. I will invite the whole town! There is a scaffold in the town square, and everyone will watch in amazement as my daughter walks into my wife's waiting arms. You must be there, boy, as a testament to your papa's character. If not, I doubt the judge will rule in his favor."

"But what if it doesn't work?" Pino asked.

"Of course it will work," Serro said. "Is your papa not the finest wood-carver in all the world?"

"Yes."

Serro smiled his cruel smile again. "I thought so. But if for some reason it doesn't work, well, you know that the scaffold has another purpose. Why, it was used only a week ago to hang a man who'd murdered his wife."

Pino held his emotions in check the whole time Geppetto was packing, not wanting to show even the slightest hint of weakness in front of Mayor Serro. And except for a bit of mist that clouded his vision as Geppetto was being driven away in the wagon, he managed to stay strong.

It was only when he returned to the cottage and found the note on the floor—where his papa must have tossed it as he was being led outside, bags in hand—that Pino finally lost his control. In a hurried scrawl the note read, "Flee! Otherwise he will kill us both, no matter what he says! And make no puppets—not for him, not for anyone! Love always, Papa."

He wept for hours after reading that note.

Finally, though, when the first light of dawn was seeping into the eastern horizon, he calmed down enough to think about the situation more clearly. He knew that Geppetto was right. The safest thing for him to do was to leave.

But what would happen to his papa?

He stood at the window and looked at the gray light spilling onto the ocean. The rippling waves made him think of the concentric circles found inside the stump of a fallen tree. He remembered how his papa had told him that those circles were a way to mark the passing of time, to know how old a tree was.

If Geppetto was to have any chance at all, it would be up to Pino. But how? He knew that creating a puppet of Serro's daughter—and he'd gotten a good enough look at that painting to know he could do it—was explicitly against his papa's wishes. So many bad things had happened because he had used his gift, and the worst of all was that he was losing his chance at being a real boy.

But was that really so terrible?

Pino had not lived a long time, but he felt like an old tree already. He felt like an old tree that was always trying to be some other kind of tree, like he was a pine when everybody else was an oak. In that moment, gazing at the rippling waves, he decided to stop trying to be a different kind of tree. He didn't know *what* kind of tree he was—there might be only one of him in the world—but whatever he was, he was just going to be that kind of tree and stop pretending.

Most importantly, he wasn't going to let his papa be killed, even if it meant Pino would turn completely back into wood.

The question was, would Serro keep his word?

CHAPTER TWENTY

When the day finally came, Pino worked right up until the very last moment, arriving at the town square when Mayor Serro was already speaking to the crowd.

During the week Pino had done his best to keep normal business going, working on his special project only at night, but with each passing day more customers were interested in only one thing: how they, too, could bring their departed loved ones back to life in puppet form. With each passing day, as he told them all no, they left more and more angry.

"Remember," Pino whispered to the child-size puppet walking next to him, its face hidden by a straw bonnet, its blue cotton dress covered with a gray shawl several sizes too large for it, "keep your head down and don't do anything until I say so."

They edged their way into the back of the crowd, Pino keeping a firm hand on the puppet's arm. Because the puppet was the size of a toddler, no one noticed its awkward, shuffling walk.

The town square overflowed with people, packed elbow to elbow between the tall brick buildings and leaning out all the windows. There were old people with canes and children on their fathers' shoulders. There was a priest in his black robes, a butcher in a spotted white apron, a schoolteacher with a dozen rosy-cheeked children in tow. A tremor of excitement ran through them all.

The sky was clear, and the sun shone so brightly that Pino had to veil his eyes to get a view of the scaffold. It was difficult to see over the old woman in front of him, but Pino got a glimpse of Mayor Serro strutting on the stage. He was dressed in the same dark suit as before, except now he wore a black top hat.

"And over here to my right," Serro was saying, his voice reedy and high but easily projecting to the farthest reaches of the crowd, "hidden under this black veil, up until this moment seen only by the master wood-carver himself, is what you have all been waiting for. In moments you will see my daughter walk amongst us again."

A murmur rippled through the crowd.

There were several people on the scaffold, seated on wooden chairs. There was indeed a child-size thing, body hidden completely by a thin black veil that draped it head to foot like a burial shroud. Next to the puppet was Geppetto, eyes downcast and hands clasped limply in his lap. On either side of him and the veiled puppet were the same two uniformed policemen who had accompanied Serro a week earlier, each clutching a rifle to his chest. Last, sitting on a chair far from the others, was what appeared to be another puppet—this one a woman in a black dress, her long white hair as fine as spider silk.

This was what Pino thought, because her skin was so pale, her body so still and frozen, her eyes so distant and vacant, that he didn't think it possible she was made out of flesh and blood. But then, as Serro went on talking about how wonderful the town was, how they would soon be famous for what they were about to see, an instant of anguish flashed across her face.

Then Pino knew: This was Serro's wife.

Towering over the scaffold, its shadow slicing the middle of the crowd like a sword, was the inverted L-shaped post where so many men and women had hanged until their bodies finally grew still and lifeless. When the mayor droned on for too long, the crowd began to grumble and shuffle. In addition to the two armed men on the scaffold, Pino counted another dozen dressed just like them scattered in the crowd.

"Now then," Serro said, "for the moment you have all been waiting for. Signore Geppetto, will you please remove the veil."

Geppetto stared at the wooden planks beneath him as if he wasn't aware that anyone else was there. The crowd fell deathly silent. The only sound was the cawing of a seabird passing overhead.

"Signore Geppetto?" Serro said, this time with more edge.

Pino wouldn't have thought it possible that his papa could slump any lower, but he did, his shoulders sagging. Without rising or even looking up, he took hold of the veil from below and gave it a feeble tug.

That was all it took. The veil slipped to the planks.

The crowd gasped. Even Pino felt his own breath catch in his throat, for the puppet—no, the child—next to his papa was an incredible likeness of the mayor's daughter, right down to the cowlick in her red hair and the daisies in her blue cotton dress. Not only had her features been carved and smoothed to perfection, her skin had been painted the exact same rosy pink.

It was a masterpiece, and for just a moment Pino forgot their perilous circumstances and felt a swelling of pride for his papa. Even Serro's wife turned to look, her eyes softening.

"Well done, sir!" Serro cried, clapping his hands. "Now, my dear Bianca, rise. Rise and come to your papa."

The puppet didn't move, just as Pino knew it wouldn't. The crowd rumbled with discontent.

"Signore?" Serro said.

Geppetto, still not looking up, let forth with a great sigh. "I told you, what you want is impossible."

Serro's jaw turned rigid. "Make her walk," he said.

"It can't be."

"Make her walk!"

The mayor's shout echoed off the brick walls. Geppetto looked up, his eyes as dead as those of his creation, but he said nothing. Serro was trembling so much Pino could see it even from where he stood. Then Pino felt it—the crowd turning, the mood shifting, the air thickening with disappointment and bitterness and rage. Serro pointed his finger at Geppetto as if it were the barrel of a gun.

"Listen carefully, wood-carver," he said, "you will make my daughter live again . . . or you will be punished for your crimes."

Pino waited, watching not Serro, Geppetto, or anyone else on the scaffold, but instead the crowd. He waited to see how they reacted. It was the one thing he needed to know.

When the crowd's reaction finally came, it came with all the force of a gale wind. The shouts and cheers crashed over Pino, raining down on him from all directions, coming from both old and young, from both men and women. He looked at their angry faces and saw not the faces of human beings, or even puppets, but the faces of the monsters that had darkened his dreams ever since his papa had been taken from him.

This reaction seemed to fill Serro with new zeal. "Well, wood-carver?" he said. "What will it be?"

Geppetto shook his head. "I have done everything I can do."

Serro paused, like a storm cloud gathering itself for a

bolt of lightning. "Then . . . you . . . will . . . *hang!*"

The crowd erupted with feverish applause and shouts of glee. Serro signaled to one of his men at the edge of the scaffold, who then climbed the steps with a noose in hand. Seeing this, the crowd cheered, the lust for violence pulsing through it like a heartbeat.

When the man reached the top step, Pino knew he could wait no longer.

"Wait!" he cried.

His voice was swallowed in the cacophony of rage. He tried again, and only the few people around him reacted, turning his way. The man with the rope, who'd already tied it to the top beam, was affixing the noose around Geppetto's neck. Pino pushed his own child puppet forward, forcing his way to the scaffold. The man with the rope prodded Geppetto to stand. Some large, sweaty men blocked Pino's way, and try as he might, he couldn't get through.

Papa was guided to a trapdoor in the center of the scaffold.

"You are hanged today," Serro said, "for murdering the innocent woman who came upon our town. If you have any last words—"

"Wait!"

The crowd, wanting to hear the mayor's remarks, had finally quieted enough for Pino to be heard. Serro searched the crowd. The people between Pino and the scaffold parted, forming an open path directly from him to the mayor. It also provided everyone up there with a clear view of Pino, including his papa.

"No!" Geppetto cried. "No, my boy! Run! Run now!"

"Ah, yes," Serro said, "the famous Pinocchio. I'd almost forgotten about you. Well, you're just in time. You, too, will hang for your father's crimes."

He signaled to the uniformed men on the outskirts of the crowd, who started immediately for him.

"No!" Geppetto cried. He tried to run toward Pino, but one of the men held him in place. "He's—he's done nothing!"

Serro didn't answer. He was squinting at the puppet standing next to Pino. "Who's that with you, boy?"

Pino had thought long and hard about what he would say in this moment, but now words deserted him. So instead he did the only thing he could do.

As the men were almost upon him, he reached out to the little puppet with his gloved hands and snatched off the bonnet and the shawl.

Gasps spread through the crowd. Serro stared with bulging eyes, and at the far end of the scaffold a strangled moan escaped the throat of his wife, who was staring at the girl in the blue dress as intensely as her husband.

For there was no question that this, indeed, was their beloved Bianca. If Geppetto's puppet had been a masterpiece, then Pino's creation was something unparalleled in the history of wood carving—a work of genius so real, so lifelike, that even standing inches away, no one in the town square that day would ever be able to look back and say this was not a real little girl. For Pino had softened the wood so that it was as pliable as flesh, found the perfect red silk for her hair, and polished the blue glass of her eyes so they shined like sapphires.

Pino bent to her dimpled cheek, his lips brushing against an ear that felt no different from a real one.

"Now," he whispered.

She bumbled forward. The crowd was so still and silent that even the soft padding of her tiny slippers on the dirt could be heard by all. When she reached the scaffold, Serro, his cheeks glistening with his tears, reached down and pulled her into his arms.

"Oh, my Bianca," he said, "oh, my dear Bianca. You've come back to us."

His wife scrambled over to them, fell, then scooted on hands and knees until she was part of their embrace. She kissed the puppet's head, and for a long while, before Pino spoke, the only sounds were the joyful sobs of a father and a mother who had been reunited with their long-lost child.

"Now let my papa go," Pino said, loud enough for all to hear. "Keep your promise."

They went on hugging and kissing the puppet as if they hadn't heard. Pino sensed the uniformed men all around him now, towering over him like the mountains.

"Let him go!" Pino shouted.

This finally seemed to get to Serro, who nodded and wiped his eyes with his sleeves. "Yes," he said. "Yes, of course. You have earned . . . have earned . . . wait. Wait, now." He leaned in, peering at the puppet's cheek, then reacted by pointing at a place where his own tears had streaked the puppet's face. "What's that? That's not flesh! That's—that's wood under there!"

Pino could not see the flaw from his distance, but he had no doubt that the paint he had so carefully applied had been partially washed away. It was, after all, only paint.

"I—I can fix—," Pino began.

"Why isn't she speaking?" Serro said. "She should be calling us Mama and Papa! Instead she only stares!"

"She can't talk," Pino admitted.

The mother was still clutching the puppet and sobbing, but Serro staggered to his feet, swaying like a drunken man.

"I want my Bianca!" Serro said. "I want her as she was!"

Pino shook his head.

"But you're a real boy!" Serro shouted. "You're just as real as the rest of us. Make her like us too!"

"I can't," Pino said.

Now the rage was returning to the crowd, seeping in from the sides like water pouring into a pit. There was angry chatter, and then someone shouted, "Hang them!"

Geppetto, who had watched this all unfold from his place on the trapdoor, the noose still around his neck, shouted, "No! Please, not my boy!"

"If I can't have one like him," Serro said, "then no one can! Bring him up here!"

The uniformed men seized Pino's arms and dragged him to the scaffold. They hoisted him up, and then one of the men up there grabbed him and brought him to the mayor.

"Please!" Geppetto cried. "Please, don't—"

The man holding Geppetto's arm slapped him hard across the face. He staggered, dazed.

"Well, Pinocchio?" Serro said. "Do you have anything to say for yourself? You are complicit in the murder of the innocent woman as well, and now you must be punished for it."

Pino swallowed. He forced himself to muster the words, because this was something he had to say. "This is your last chance," he said. "Let my papa go . . . or else."

Most of the crowd laughed, as did the mayor.

"Or else?" he said. "Or else what?"

Pino looked over at the crowd, raising his voice so that no one could mistake his words. "If you don't want to be hurt," he warned, "you must go now."

This time the laughter was louder. Whether it was Pino's

warning, or simply that they did not want to witness the hanging of a boy, however, many people did leave—the teacher with her class, many mothers and their children, the priests, some of the elderly. Much to Pino's disappointment, though, many remained, and those who did looked at him with renewed hate. Pino wondered why there was so much cruelness in this town.

"I've changed my mind!" Serro said gleefully. "Let the boy hang first!"

"No!" Geppetto cried.

The noose was removed, and it took two men to do it, tussling with Geppetto as they dragged him, screaming, away from the trapdoor. One of the men grabbed Pino.

"Wait," a small voice said, so small that Pino thought perhaps a miracle had happened and it was the puppet speaking after all.

But when he looked, he saw that it was the mother, gazing up at Serro with a face red from crying. "Wait," she said, "don't do this. He's only a boy."

"No, he's not," Serro said. "He's—he's something wicked."

"We have our Bianca. Let them go."

"She's not Bianca!"

"Yes she is! She's our daughter. Look at her! She's come back to us. She—"

"Silence!" Serro cried.

He seized Pino's arm himself and positioned him on the trapdoor, then slipped the noose over his neck. It felt as coarse as bark.

With the noose sufficiently tight, the mayor signaled to a man at the far end who stood by a lever. When the man reached for the lever, Pino knew that he had to act. He'd given these people every chance to do what was right.

He formed his lips into an O and blew as hard as he could. Whistling was not something he'd ever done well before now, but he'd been practicing all week, and the sound was clear and penetrating. He whistled with all his heart—whistled just the way his papa had told him to whistle when he wanted help. It was a sound that could be heard all over town.

The mayor, the crowd, the man with the lever—everyone froze. As the whistle faded, Pino looked at Geppetto, whose own anguish only deepened. Still restrained by the uniformed men, he reached feebly for Pino.

"What nonsense is this?" Serro said. "Are you . . ."

He trailed off because another sound had filled the square. It was a dull thudding, a clopping that echoed off the bricks, a clacking that repeated itself many times.

It was the sound of wooden footsteps.

A woman screamed before Pino saw them, and then another, and then there was screaming from all around. The crowd stampeded in all directions. Pino finally saw them: dozens upon dozens of wooden puppets marching into the town square from every direction.

They were crude, these things, these monsters that Pino had formed from whatever he could find. They were made of broom handles and desk drawers and roof shingles. They were made of toy boats and bedposts and soup bowls. They had not been made to bring someone's loved one back from the dead, or to allow a crippled person to walk, or to give a scarred woman a chance to see her beauty again.

In fact, there was no beauty in these puppets at all, and yet they had been made with the greatest amount of love a wood-carver could bring to his work. They had been made with only one purpose in mind—to cause as much panic in those they encountered as possible. And that they did. They did it as well as it could be done. They swung their bulky arms and kicked their bulky feet, and people fled in fear. It was the first time Pino had created something that had done exactly as he had intended it to do.

Serro finally came to his senses enough to shout at the man with the lever. "Pull it!"

The man hesitated, then shook his head and ran, stumbling down into the fleeing mass of bodies.

Cursing, Serro started for the lever, but then he cried out in surprise. The puppet of the mayor's daughter had bitten into his ankle, and her jaw was as strong as a metal trap, just as Pino had made it to be.

Serro beat and flailed at the puppet to no avail, and then his sobbing wife threw herself on him. They rolled off the scaffold, directly into the path of the wooden monstrosities marching their way. What became of them Pino never knew, because he felt the noose lift from around his neck and someone tug his hand in the opposite direction.

"Come, son," Geppetto said.

He turned and saw his papa's face, and it was not relief or anger that he saw there, but something else altogether. He didn't understand. In the melee no one tried to stop them from fleeing—and Pino directed his papa to the big ships down by the docks. Planning for this moment, he had already booked passage on a great vessel that was leaving shortly.

They did not stop running. They did not look back. They ran until they'd reached the big ship with its big sails, until they'd scurried up the gangplank and stood with their hands on the rails, gasping for breath. They couldn't have timed their escape better, for within minutes the ropes were tossed aboard, the sails were unfurled, and the big ship tilted and rocked as it churned the waters, heading out to sea.

As the land slowly receded, the mountains shrinking before him, Pino turned to Geppetto. Again there was this strange look in Geppetto's eyes.

"What is it, Papa?" he asked.

"It's nothing," Geppetto said. "You're just . . ." Then he looked down and pointed with amazement at Pino's gloved hands. In all the action, the cloth had been ripped, and the skin visible underneath wasn't wood—it was flesh. "My word!" he exclaimed.

Pino ripped off what remained of the gloves and pulled up both sleeves. Sure enough, there was no part of him that was not flesh as real as flesh could be. "But why?" he said. "I used my gift! And I—I did something terrible."

Geppetto clapped his son on the shoulder. "Do you think what you did was wrong?"

Pino considered. "No," he replied. "Awful, yes. But . . . not wrong."

"Would you do it again?"

Pino tried to hold the tears back, but it was difficult. He did not like doing something awful, even when he had no choice. "If I had to, Papa. Only if I had to."

Geppetto made no effort to hold back his own tears. "Oh, my dear boy. *That* is what I was going to tell you a moment ago—why I look at you so differently now. You're just not my little Pino anymore. I already see in you the man you will become."

"But I'll never be a real man!" Pino protested. "I'm not even a real boy! I'll always be different. I know that now."

"Yes, yes, exactly!" Geppetto said. "Don't you see? I was

wrong too. You weren't turning into wood because you were using your gift. You were turning into wood because you were trying to be something you weren't. Whether you are like other boys or not, what does it matter, so long as you accept yourself the way you are? You can be different *and* real, Pino. You can be both."

It was then, watching the land vanish into the mist that crowded the shores, that Pino finally understood. He understood because he remembered what the voice in the cave had told him.

As long as you are true to yourself, your heart will never harden, and the future is yours to shape.

It made him smile, thinking this, and he didn't care if it was a real boy's smile or not. It was just a smile and it was good. He took his papa's hand, and together they turned, the wind blowing back their hair, the sun bright in their eyes, and squinted at all the ocean that lay before them. Somewhere beyond that ocean their new home awaited. Pino couldn't see it yet, but he knew it was out there.

He was ready for it.

ABOUT THE AUTHOR

Scott William Carter's first novel, *The Last Great Getaway of the Water Balloon Boys*, was hailed by *Publishers Weekly* as a "touching and impressive debut." His short stories have appeared in dozens of popular magazines and anthologies. He lives in Oregon with his wife, two children, and thousands of imaginary friends. Read more about his books for younger readers at rymadoon.com.